Does Christina have a new enemy?

"You should have told me Sterling chewed." Eliza's face was white with anger.

"I didn't know she did," Christina replied. "At home we keep our stuff in a tack room."

Eliza frowned. "Well, I guess we don't have the fancy setup you have. If your horse is the type that grabs other people's tack, you should have brought a stall guard to keep her head in."

"I'm sorry," Christina said, reaching for the rein Sterling had chewed. It was bent in two places, but it wasn't damaged to the point that it would break. "If I rubbed Neatsfoot oil into it, you'd hardly be able to see where she chewed."

Eliza snatched the rein back. "You've done enough damage already."

"Suit yourself," Christina snapped, out of patience. "But if you had put the bridle in your tack trunk instead of letting it hang outside, Sterling wouldn't have been able to get it in the first place."

Eliza gave her a disgusted look and turned away.

"I'll go to the tack shop down the road and buy a stall guard tomorrow," Christina said as she turned to leave.

Christina heard Eliza mutter something about spoiled rich kids, but she kept walking. She was too tired to fight anymore.

THOROUGHBRED

CAMP SADDLEBROOK

CREATED BY
JOANNA CAMPBELL

WRITTEN BY
DALE GASQUE

HarperPaperbacks
A Division of HarperCollinsPublishers

HarperPaperbacks
A Division of HarperCollins*Publishers*
10 East 53rd Street, New York, NY 10022-5299

This is a work of fiction. The characters, incidents, and dialogues are products of the author's imagination and are not to be construed as real. Any resemblance to actual events or persons, living or dead, is entirely coincidental.

ISBN 0-06-106530-7

First printing: July 1998

Printed in the United States of America

Visit HarperPaperbacks on the World Wide Web at
http://www.harpercollins.com

❖ 10 9 8 7 6 5 4 3 2

CAMP
SADDLEBROOK

"WOW. CHECK OUT THOSE JUMPS." CHRISTINA REESE pressed her nose against the truck window and watched a field dotted with cross-country fences whiz by.

Her cousin, Melanie Graham, leaned across Christina to get a closer look. "Awesome. Do you think we're going to jump any like that?"

"I hope so." Christina shivered with excitement. The girls were on their way to a three-week-long riding camp at Saddlebrook Farm, training ground of some of the best event riders in the United States. Christina couldn't wait to get there.

Melanie ran a hand through her short, light blond hair. "I hope I'm good enough to do this eventing stuff."

"You'll be fine," Christina said, grinning at her cousin. "Don't forget that you and Trib rode a better dressage test at Mona's show than I did."

1

The girls would both be entering eighth grade in the fall, but they didn't look the same age at all. Melanie was slender and petite, and Christina was tall and long legged with an athletic build. Melanie was a pretty good match in both size and temperament for Christina's tiny, feisty pony, Tribulation.

Christina twisted her strawberry blond ponytail around her finger and continued staring out the window, thinking about the recent dressage show at her riding instructor's farm. Sterling Dream, Christina's new horse, had gone around the ring as if she were on the racetrack, where she had spent the first few years of her life. It was discouraging, but Christina wasn't about to give up. She was certain the mare had the heart and talent to do all three phases of eventing: dressage, cross-country, and show jumping.

"I'm worried about riding Trib cross-country," Melanie said, sliding down in the seat and propping her feet up on the truck's dashboard.

"Hey." Joe Kisner took one hand off the steering wheel and swatted at Melanie's sneakers. Christina giggled as Melanie squirmed away. "Look what you did," he said, motioning to the powdery brown tread marks from her shoes.

Joe was one of the grooms who worked for Christina's parents at Whitebrook, the Reeses' Thoroughbred training and breeding farm. He was driving them to the camp because Christina's parents were busy taking some three-year-old horses to the racetrack. It wasn't always easy being the only child of Ashleigh Griffen, the Kentucky Derby–winning jockey, and Michael Reese, one of the most respected Thoroughbred trainers in the country. Sometimes Christina wondered what it would be like to have parents who came home at night after regular jobs. But then she and Sterling might not be on the way to their first overnight riding camp.

"This is it," Joe said as he turned the pickup truck and horse trailer onto the long, tree-lined driveway of Saddlebrook Farm. Even though the windows were rolled up and the air-conditioning was blasting, Christina could hear Sterling's and Trib's high-pitched whinnies coming from the trailer.

Melanie nudged Christina with her elbow. "Camp Saddlebrook, here we come," she said with a grin.

Christina could hardly keep from bouncing up and down like an excited three-year-old. She strained forward against her seat belt to check the place out.

Joe was taking it easy on the gravel driveway so that the horses wouldn't get bumped around. Christina peeked through the trees on the right and saw a dressage ring with white chains looping from one boxed letter to the next to form a fence about a foot off the ground.

Coming up on the left was a large oval ring filled with brightly painted jumps. Christina got even more excited. Dressage was okay, but there was nothing she liked better than flying over a fence on a horse. As they drove past the ring, Christina twisted in her seat, her eyes on the big green oxer. She was picturing herself cantering Sterling toward the jump when Melanie's voice interrupted.

"Get a load of that house." Her cousin drew her breath back in a whistle. "Not too shabby."

The avenue of trees had grown wider as the driveway split, forming a circle in front of a huge white farmhouse surrounded by a porch big enough to ride a horse around. Christina's stomach fluttered with butterflies. They were finally here.

"I hope we're in time for mint juleps on the veranda," Melanie said in a fake southern accent.

Christina giggled. Even though she hadn't been crazy at first about having Melanie come stay with her family for the summer, they had become good friends after a slightly rocky start.

When Melanie first came to Kentucky from New York City, where she lived with her father and a series of housekeepers, she would hardly talk to anyone. Christina knew it was because of a terrible accident in which her favorite horse had been hit by a taxi. Since Melanie's mom had died when she was little, and her father, Christina's Uncle Will, was out of town a lot with his recording business, he had sent Melanie to Whitebrook Farm to recover from the trauma and to stay out of trouble. Melanie claimed he was just looking for an excuse to get rid of her.

Joe took the fork to the right past a neatly mowed

4

green with two long barns on either side and a flagpole in the middle that was surrounded by flowers. A smaller shed that was stuffed with hay and flanked by two trees completed the horseshoe shape. Christina counted twelve stalls in each barn, twenty-four in all. The tops of the stalls' Dutch doors were hooked back and the bottoms were trimmed with crossed white boards so that they looked like a row of ticktacktoe squares. Some of the stalls were already occupied, and curious faces with ears pricked forward watched the parade of wheelbarrows and tack trunks as campers and parents bustled about.

The roof of each building sloped out in front to form a wide aisle. On the other side of the aisle, horses and ponies of all sizes were tied along the dirt alleyway that separated the barn from the green. Some girls stood on buckets as they evened their horses' manes. Others brushed necks and hindquarters that were already gleaming with elbow grease. Christina wished she hadn't taken so long to pack. It looked as if they were the last ones here.

"Is that Dakota?" Melanie said, leaning over Christina again as she peered out the window.

Christina's heart skipped a beat before she realized that the chestnut her cousin was pointing to was smaller than the quarter horse that belonged to Dylan Becker, a friend from home who took lessons from the same instructor as Melanie and Christina. "No," Christina said, searching the crowd for her friend. Or boyfriend, as Melanie would say, but Christina wasn't comfortable with the boyfriend-girlfriend thing and didn't think of him that way. She did like hanging out with him, though. Dylan was as crazy about horses as she was. Of course, it didn't hurt that he was cute, too.

Two girls who looked as though they were in high school stepped into the driveway and signaled Joe to stop. One of them peered into the truck as Joe rolled down the window.

"Hi. Welcome to Saddlebrook. Two campers, huh? What are your names?"

"Melanie Graham and Christina Reese," Melanie said before Christina could open her mouth.

"We heard you were coming. Bring any Triple Crown winners with you?" the girl joked as she consulted her clipboard. "You're in A Barn with Dana." She waved her arm toward the other girl, who was already starting back toward the trailer. "That's Dana and I'm Adrianne. May I see your horses' health papers?"

"They're in my tack trunk," Christina said, half out of the truck. The warm, damp air pressed into her like a blanket when she emerged from the air-conditioning. "I'll get them."

The trailer was extra long because it had a separate dressing room compartment in front of the horses. Before Christina went into the dressing room to get the papers, though, she wanted to reassure Sterling. The mare was sometimes fearful of strangers, no doubt because a groom had badly mistreated her at the racetrack before Christina bought her. As she reached for the handle, she could hear Sterling scrambling inside. "Coming in," Christina said to warn Sterling.

But it was too late. Sterling already had her head up and was pulling back against the nylon ties that kept her from turning around in the narrow stall. Her eyes were rolled back as she snorted at Dana, who had entered the trailer from the door on the other side.

"Easy, girl," Christina said, putting a hand on the mare's sweaty neck and talking to her until she relaxed. She smiled at Dana. "Sterling gets spooked if you walk in on her without a warning."

"That's a Thoroughbred for you," Dana said, shaking her head. "More nerves than brains."

Christina stared at Dana to see if she was joking, but the older girl's mouth was pulled back in disdain. Christina bristled. "Thoroughbreds are fine if you know how to handle them."

Dana looked at her coolly before dropping her eyes to the sheet on the clipboard. "Name?"

"Reese. Christina."

Adrianne popped her head in the door. "Hello, cuties," she said when Sterling and Trib turned her way. "I told your dad where to unload."

Christina was puzzled for a second, then laughed. "Joe's not my father," she said. "He just works for us."

When Dana shot Adrianne a look, Christina realized how snobby that must have sounded.

"He looks after the farm when my parents are at the racetrack," she explained.

Adrianne smiled. "It must be exciting to be Ashleigh Griffen's daughter."

"Not really," Christina said, shrugging. "I'm not into racing the way she and my father are."

Once the health papers were checked, Joe pulled into the parking lot behind the stable area, expertly backing the trailer into an open space.

"Don't you wish we'd gotten assigned to Adrianne's barn?" Christina asked.

Melanie blew a bubble so big she had to pop it with her finger before she could get the gum back in her mouth. "Yeah. Dana looks like she sucks on lemons."

Christina laughed.

Since Joe had to get back to the farm to help with evening chores, they unloaded the tack and stable equipment right away. "I'll be right back," Christina told Sterling as she struggled to hold up one end of the trunk she'd gotten from her parents for Christmas. Its burnished gold wood held all of Sterling's stuff—saddle, bridle, grooming kit, fly sheet, cooling sheet, leg wraps, shampoo, first-aid kit, plus Christina's helmet, gloves, and boots—neatly separated with dividers and trays. It even had a brass plate with her name engraved on it screwed into the top.

"What did you put in here?" Joe teased. "The washroom sink?"

Christina slapped her hand to her forehead. *"That's* what I forgot."

"Where am I going?" Melanie called back. She was carrying a saddle on one arm and a bridle and bucket on the other.

"Adrianne said A Barn." Christina nodded at the barn on the left. "I bet it's that one."

They had to stop a bunch of times before Christina's trunk was finally in place outside of her assigned stall. "I don't know how Sterling's going to like it here," she said, peeking over the door. "This is tiny compared to the stalls at home."

Melanie set her saddle down on the railing and glanced into Trib's stall, which was just to the left of Sterling's. "Less to clean," she pointed out.

"Speaking of cleaning," Joe said, heading back to the trailer for another load, "you two better get a move on bedding down these stalls so I can unload the horses and get out of here."

Christina and Melanie followed him. Sterling got a quick pat before Christina wrestled the wheelbarrow out of the trailer's narrow dressing room door while Joe and Melanie carried the other tack trunk. A lot of riding groups rented Saddlebrook Farm for shows and clinics, but everyone had to bring their own tools. She piled the rakes, pitchforks, and feed buckets into the wheelbarrow before pushing the precarious lot across the bumpy parking lot. The rake on top kept bouncing off.

"Man, is it hot," she complained when she finally reached the stalls.

Melanie was rummaging through the black trunk she'd borrowed from Whitebrook Farm. "Catch," she said, pulling a soda can out and tossing it over to Christina.

"Thanks." Christina popped the lid and took a long drink. Even though it was warm, it felt good going down her dry throat. She took another swig and watched a tall girl with a long, fat blond braid over one shoulder stagger under the weight of a plastic muck bucket piled high with sawdust. The girl stopped at the last stall in the barn, just to the right of Sterling's.

"Excuse me," Christina said. "Where do we get the bedding?"

"Behind the hay barn, in the shed." The girl glanced at Christina's trunk.

"Thanks." Christina hesitated, then added, "My name's Christina Reese."

The girl nodded her head. "I figured you were the one."

"What?"

"That they're *bending* the rules for," she said, flipping her braid back.

Christina could feel her face get red. "What are you talking about?"

"Your horse is only four, right?"

"Yeah," Christina answered, wondering how she knew.

"You're not supposed to bring horses younger than five to the camp." The girl opened the latch of her stall before adding, "But I guess it depends on who your parents are. Back up, bud."

The black horse moved away from the opening as the girl dragged the muck bucket into the stall. She closed the door behind her without giving Christina another look.

"What business is it of hers how old Sterling is?" Christina said with an embarrassed laugh as she turned toward her cousin. "We're all here to learn."

Melanie shrugged, looking just as surprised as Christina felt.

Twenty minutes later, both stalls were bedded and ready. Christina leaned the rake against her trunk and swept the loose hairs off her sweaty forehead. "I hope Sterling appreciates the extra sawdust I put in." She looked around, trying to spot Dylan in the busy aisles. Maybe he wasn't here yet. She hoped he wasn't assigned to the other barn.

When the girl with the braid came out of her horse's stall, she looked past Christina as though she weren't even there. "Jennifer!"

"Hey, Eliza," said the girl whose stall was on the other side of Melanie's. With her large dark eyes, boyish haircut, and size one body, she looked like a model out of a *Delia's* catalog. She gave Christina a quick smile as she walked toward the girl with the braid—Eliza. "New horse?"

Eliza hesitated a second before saying, "Meet Flash."

Jennifer stood on tiptoe as she peered over the door. "Wow. How big is he?"

"Sixteen-two," Eliza said. "Did you bring Geronimo?"

"Who else? Hey, did you see who's a junior instructor this year?" Jennifer had a surprisingly deep laugh.

Eliza rolled her eyes. "You mean Dana?"

"Yeah." Jennifer helped Eliza put her rake and pitchfork into the muck bucket. "We should try to be instructors next year."

"You have to be at least sixteen," Eliza said. "I won't be fifteen until this October."

"Bummer. I won't be old enough next summer, either."

"Chris!" Melanie shouted from the edge of the parking lot. "Joe says to move your butt."

As Christina scooted by Eliza and Jennifer, she hoped her cheeks just looked red from the heat.

As soon as Christina backed Sterling out of the trailer, the mare started prancing, her head turning from side to side as she arched her neck and called to the other horses. "Settle down," Christina said, giving the lead line a sharp tug to get Sterling's attention. The mare walked a few steps before planting her feet and whinnying again. Christina could see the veins standing out under her thin, quivering skin.

"Hurry up," Christina called to Melanie. Sterling would be a lot easier to control once Trib was beside her. Racehorses were used to being accompanied by their "ponies"—older and calmer horses that they followed out to the track.

"Keep your shirt on, Cuz," Melanie said as Trib's brown-and-white hindquarters appeared. Trib took short, careful steps as he backed down the trailer ramp before looking around. Melanie had her arm draped across his neck, and for a second, Christina was jealous. Even though Trib could be a pain sometimes under saddle, at least he was calm and had a cool head in strange places.

As soon as Trib was beside her, Sterling relaxed enough to walk without pulling Christina's arm out of its socket. Melanie led the way. As Christina followed, she started to enjoy the fact that she was leading a flashy young Thoroughbred. Sterling's silver dapples positively gleamed as the sunlight bounced off her back. She might not be the best-trained horse at camp, but Christina bet her mare would turn the most heads.

When they got to the stalls, Christina and Melanie tied Trib and Sterling to the fence in front of the barn so that they could remove the shipping boots that protected the horses' legs when they were in the trailer. Melanie was already chatting away with Jennifer. They had found something in common right away since Jennifer's horse, Geronimo, was a pinto, too.

"We'll probably be together in the kennel," Jennifer told them, "since our stalls are next to each other. They usually assign the cabins by team."

"We're sleeping with dogs?" Melanie had a horrified look on her face.

Jennifer laughed. "No. The building used to be the foxhound kennel for the hunt before it was converted into cabins. The name just stuck."

"How many kids will be on our team?" Christina asked, tossing Sterling's front boots into the top of her trunk.

"Four." Jennifer pointed toward Flash's stall and counted. "Eliza, you, Melanie, and me—they do it by stalls."

Great, Christina thought, taking Sterling's right hind boot off and running her hand along the mare's hindquarters as she crossed around to the other side so that Sterling would know she was there. *It's bad enough not to be on the same team with Dylan without having to room with that snob, Eliza.*

As she bent to pull the Velcro tabs open on Sterling's left hind boot, the mare snorted and jerked back so far her haunches nearly touched the ground. At the same moment, she heard the sound of splintering wood.

"Watch out," Melanie yelled.

A piece of board flew past Christina's face. She ducked out of the way just as Sterling swung around, the lead line whipping Christina's cheek.

"Whoa," Christina shouted, but it was too late. The mare shot across the green toward the other barn, her back leg kicking at the dangling shipping boot as if it were a rattlesnake.

2

"Whoa," Christina shouted again as she ran after Sterling.

"Loose horse, hold the others," a sharp British voice called out. Kids scurried to the horses that were tied along the rails so that they wouldn't panic and pull back, too.

"Block the driveway, please, and don't run."

Sterling swerved away from the people who positioned themselves at the end of the green, waving their arms to shoo her away from the driveway. As she wheeled around, one back foot stepped on the flopping boot on the other back foot and tore it off. Now that she was rid of the horrible, hanging thing, Sterling's tail shot up into the air. The long black hairs streamed behind her like a flag as she slowed from her breakneck gallop to an animated trot.

17

"Nice piaffe," someone called, mentioning a movement from dressage.

"You mean passage," another kid answered. "She's not staying in the same spot."

"Come here, girl," Christina cooed, holding out her hand as if she had a carrot. But Sterling was too smart to fall for that old trick. She tossed her head and wheeled to the right, obviously enjoying her new-found freedom.

"All right! A turn on the haunches. Maybe she'll do aires above the ground next."

Christina flushed. This was *not* the sort of attention she wanted.

"Enough chatter, kids," the British voice commanded. Christina glanced to the right and saw a woman in tan breeches and black boots striding toward Sterling. "Come along now. You've had your fun."

Sterling was nose to nose with a roan pony tied to the fence by the other barn. She squealed and was about to turn away when the woman caught up to her. "Here, now. That's enough nonsense for today," the woman said, laying one hand on the mare's neck and reaching for the lead line with the other. After giving her a quick pat, she turned. "To whom does this horse belong?"

Christina felt everyone's eyes on her as she jogged forward. "I'm sorry," she said. "Sterling doesn't usually pull away like that."

18

The woman looked older up close. When she smiled, the lines around her eyes crinkled together. "Not to worry. We'll be doing quite well if only one horse escapes each day."

"Ms. Perkins," someone called. "Can you help me find Mushroom's pulse?"

"In a moment," the woman answered. She turned back to Christina. "I don't believe I recognize your face."

Christina shook her head. "This is my first time here. I'm Christina Reese."

The woman stretched out her hand. "Ms. Perkins," she said, introducing herself. "Though sometimes they call me Perky—not to my face, of course. Terrible name, that. Makes me think of a coffee pot."

Christina laughed. Ms. Perkins didn't seem as forbidding as she sounded with her proper English accent.

"Run along now and finish your chores. You don't want to lose points on your first inspection," Ms. Perkins said, already walking toward the girl who was waving from a stall.

Christina felt better as she led Sterling back to A Barn. "Give me a heart attack, why don't you," she murmured to the mare, more relieved than mad. What if something had happened to her?

Dana scowled as Christina approached. She had a piece of wood in her hand.

"Rule one. *Never* tie a horse to a fence board. You're lucky it didn't hit someone in the head when she pulled back like that."

Christina frowned. "But all the others are tied that way," she protested. "Besides, I used a release knot."

"That only works if you're right there when the horse starts pulling," Dana said, rolling her eyes. "If you had tied her to the piece of baling twine, it would have broken when she got scared and pulled."

Christina looked around. Sure enough, the lead lines of the horses that were tied along the rail were looped through circles of cheap twine that came off bales of hay. Why hadn't she noticed that before?

"Now I've got to find Gus and tell him the fence is broken. He's not going to be very happy." Dana stomped off, shaking her head.

"You okay, Cuz?" Melanie asked with a sympathetic look as she came out of Trib's stall.

"Yeah, I guess."

Eliza came out of Flash's stall with her grooming kit. "Nice job," she said with a baleful look. "That'll cost our team some points."

"Sorry," Christina said with a shrug, determined not to let Eliza see she was upset. "At home, we always put the horses on crossties in the aisle when we have them out of their stalls."

"We don't *care* how you do things at home," Eliza said. "The sooner you get that into your head, the better."

Christina's heart was hammering as she led Sterling into her stall. What was Eliza's problem? She started to run her hands along Sterling's legs to see if the mare had done any damage during her run.

"About time you got here."

Christina peeked over the door to see who Melanie was teasing. Dylan was leading Dakota with one hand and balancing a saddle on his arm with the other. He looked totally cool in his cutoffs, T-shirt, and baseball cap turned backward.

She reached over the stall door and let herself out. "Hey, Dylan."

Dylan squinted as he looked around. "Hey, Chris," he said, breaking into a wide grin. He stopped Dakota and shifted the saddle to his other arm. "I guess this means I'm not in the same barn as you guys."

Christina wrinkled her nose. "What barn are you assigned to?"

"B Barn. Over there."

"She knows all about B Barn," Melanie said, carrying a water bucket up to the spigot. "She and Sterling have already explored the place."

Dylan raised his eyebrows. "Oh yeah?"

Christina frowned, shoving her hands in the back pockets of her cutoffs. "Don't even ask," she said, leaning against Sterling's door and getting ready to tell him about their escapade.

But Dylan's eyes shifted away. "I better get going.

We had a flat tire on the way up, so I'm just getting unloaded. I'll see you at dinner."

Christina sighed as she watched him cross the green. Kids were calling out to him as he walked by.

"Hey, Dylan. We were afraid you weren't coming this year."

"Your stall is next to mine, right on the end."

"Hey, man. I was wondering if I was going to have all these girls to myself." This last comment came from a boy with longish blond hair and sunglasses, who only came up to Dylan's shoulder.

Dylan laughed, but Christina couldn't hear his answer and she went back into Sterling's stall.

"You almost finished?" Melanie asked. "Jennifer and I are going to the kennel."

Christina glanced at the blood on her fingers from the scratch she'd found on Sterling's inside hind leg. "I have to clean this cut and put some antibiotic ointment on it first."

Melanie shrugged. "Okay. See you in a few minutes." Christina could hear her laughing with Jennifer as they left the barn area.

"They could have waited," she said under her breath as she rummaged through her tack trunk for the first-aid kit. She tensed up as Eliza came out of her horse's stall, but the girl just walked by without a word.

Christina was sticky and grimy when she finally finished with Sterling. She pulled her T-shirt away from her sweaty skin as she left the barn and walked by herself past the big house. Some campers were sitting in rocking chairs with their feet propped up on the porch railing. "Hi," Christina said, but they were talking too loudly to hear her.

She dropped her eyes and pretended she was in a hurry. If only her best friend from home, Katie, hadn't had to visit her sick grandmother in California. Until a couple of days ago, Katie was supposed to come to the camp, too. Katie wouldn't have run off and left Christina by herself. She kicked at a rock lying in the dirt just as she reached the kennel.

The kennel was a long, narrow building with an overhang like the barns. But instead of Dutch doors like the stalls, there were six screened doors evenly spaced down the front. In between each door were two square windows with screens instead of glass.

Christina peeked through the screen of the first door into a small room, but all the beds were already made and no one was inside. In the second room, someone was standing by one of the bunk beds. Christina felt like a Peeping Tom and was about to back away when she spotted her footlocker. This was her room.

She resisted the temptation to knock and pulled the screen door open. The room was dim after the bright afternoon light. It took a second before she recognized Eliza's long, thick braid.

Eliza glanced over her shoulder, then turned back

to the top bunk where she was putting on sheets. "You're on the bottom."

"Okay," Christina said, determined not to let Eliza get to her, though truthfully she would much rather have had the top bunk.

Christina looked at the other bunk and saw Melanie's old quilt hanging over the top. Darn that Sterling, anyway. If she hadn't freaked and gotten loose, Christina wouldn't have been stuck with the last bed.

She shoved her footlocker until it was next to the iron bed. Besides the four footlockers and two bunks, the room was empty.

"Where do we put our clothes?"

"In your trunk," Eliza said as if she were talking to someone who wasn't very bright.

Christina thought about her room at home with the closet big enough to fit her dresser, too. Oh, well. At least she had plenty of space in her trunk. When she bent down to open the latches, she caught a glimpse of her hands. Yuck. She looked around. "Where's the bathroom?"

"Out back."

Great, Christina thought as she followed the path up the hill. *I hope I don't have to pee in the middle of the night.*

The bathroom wasn't as bad as Christina thought it might be. There were stalls for the toilets just like at school, and the showers had wooden doors instead of curtains that might accidentally blow open. Christina had worried for a second that it would be like a locker room where you had to take showers in front of everyone.

By the time she got back to the cabin, Eliza was gone. She could hear a lot of kids laughing further down the kennel. Melanie was probably clowning around right in the middle. Christina looked at the drab wood walls of their cabin. Too bad she hadn't thought to bring any posters. Oh, well. At least the place would look brighter when she made up her bed.

As Christina spread the sheets over her bed, she remembered the shopping trip she'd taken with her mother when they'd bought the T-shirts and underwear and stuff she needed for camp. Melanie didn't want to go, so it was just the two of them. They left right after evening chores and grabbed dinner at the mall. Usually her mom didn't like to shop, but that night as they went from store to store they ended up with almost more than they could carry.

"It's the first time you've ever gone away by yourself," her mother had said. "I just want to make sure you have everything you need." She laughed when she added, "This way, we won't have to buy as much when you go to college." And later on when she put her arm around Christina's waist she said, "I can't believe you're taller than I am now. Stop growing up so fast."

All of a sudden, Christina was homesick for her

mom and dad. Even for the stupid pink room she'd outgrown. As she smoothed the mossy green sheets and pulled up the Aztec-print comforter she and her mom had picked out, Christina wondered what her parents were doing right now. Probably feeding the horses.

The horses! Christina's heart plummeted when she looked at her watch. Ten minutes after five. She was supposed to have been back in the barn to feed Sterling ten minutes ago.

What was Dana going to say now?

3

CHRISTINA WAS OUT OF BREATH AS SHE RAN ALONG THE gravel in front of A Barn. She could see Sterling's elegant head hanging over the door, her black-tipped ears pricked forward as she waited for supper. The mare whinnied and banged the stall door with her front foot as Christina ducked under the rail.

"I know, I know. You want your dinner." Christina stopped a second to rub Sterling. The silver dapples on the mare's cheeks faded to a rosy gray on her nose. "I'd better put some sunscreen on you tomorrow," Christina said, planting a quick kiss on the velvety, sunburned snip on her muzzle before turning away to get the grain.

The small yellow bucket she'd brought for carrying grain wasn't in the extra water bucket. She could have sworn she'd left it there. Her eyes shifted to

Flash's stall, but Eliza wasn't in sight. Was she the sort of person who'd take things to make trouble?

Christina dug through her tack trunk, but it wasn't in there, either. She ended up dumping her saddle soap, tack sponge, and polish out of the cleaning bucket and heading to the feed room with that. She was in such a hurry that she almost bumped into Melanie.

"Slow down, Cuz." Melanie held up the missing yellow bucket. "I got Sterling's feed for you before she kicked her door down. You've got one impatient mare."

"Thanks a million." Christina flashed Melanie a smile as she took the grain. "I was afraid Dana would find one more thing to gripe about. She's even pickier than my mom."

Melanie's eyes widened and she pushed into Christina, almost spilling the feed.

"What did you do that—" Christina broke off when she realized who was behind her.

"Hi, Dana," Melanie said in a singsong voice. She giggled as she grabbed Christina and ran. "Boy, she's ugly when she's mad."

A deep bell sounded just as Christina was raking the aisle in front of Sterling's stall. Melanie and Jennifer had already finished. Christina glanced at Flash's stall. Since she was going to be stuck with Eliza for the next three weeks, maybe she should try to be friendly.

"Was that the dinner bell?" she asked as Eliza brushed invisible dirt off her horse's gleaming flanks.

Eliza glanced up. "Five-minute warning."

"His coat is beautiful," Christina said, admiring Flash's sheen. "What supplements do you use?"

"Just hay, grain, and a lot of brushing." Eliza ducked under his neck to the other side.

"Really? We spend a lot on special vitamins and stuff, but I don't think any of our horses have coats like that."

Eliza didn't say anything as she squatted and ran the brush down one of Flash's white stockings, so Christina tried again.

"He's a Thoroughbred, isn't he?"

"Yeah."

"Sterling is, too. She's off the track. Did Flash ever race?"

"For a few years." Eliza moved to Flash's tail, her fingers letting a few hairs escape at a time as she ran the brush through.

"Do you event him?"

"I've been competing him at training level this summer. He'll be ready to go preliminary in the fall."

Christina figured Eliza must be a pretty good rider. Training level didn't sound very advanced, but she knew that it was more than most riders could handle. It was one thing to jump three and a half feet in a flat ring as hunters do at horse shows, and another thing altogether to gallop up and down hills jumping fences your horse has never seen before. And even though training-level event fences were only three feet, three inches maximum, they were built out of solid things such as telephone poles or hay wagons up to five feet wide. Maybe Eliza would give her some pointers with Sterling.

"Look," Eliza said, stopping brushing long enough to give Christina a cool stare. "I'm going to stay out here a little longer, so don't wait for me."

"Okay," Christina said. "See you up there." She tried to sound matter-of-fact to hide her disappointment. Eliza seemed determined to keep her at a distance.

Everyone else must be in the house already, Christina thought as she walked down the empty aisle of A Barn, stopping at a few doors to say hello to some friendly horses. *B Barn looked deserted, too, so Dylan must already be inside.*

As Christina climbed the front steps to the house, she could hear laughter inside. She stopped at the pile of sneakers and boots scattered along the rail of the porch and added her own to the bunch. Her socks had a ring of brown where the tops of her shoes had been, so she stripped them off. Then she took a deep breath and followed the noise.

The side door opened to a little hall with a sink and counter on one side and a bulletin board on the other. Christina skimmed a few notices of horses for sale and upcoming shows before turning to wash her hands. She glanced at the mirror above the sink and rubbed at the brown streaks of dirt that made her face look even more freckled than usual. Wisps of frizzy hairs that were too short to stay tied up curled in a damp fringe around her forehead. She wished her hair was straight like Melanie's.

After she splashed water on her face and neck and dried herself with a paper towel, she looked back in the mirror. Hazel eyes stared back as she tried a smile. So what if things were a little rocky at first? She'd feel better after she talked to Dylan.

"Where were you?" Melanie said, waving as Christina found her way to a room that was almost completely filled by the longest picnic table she had ever seen.

Melanie scooted over on the bench to make room and Dylan smiled and nodded to her from the other side. Platters with hamburgers and hot dogs were circling the table as excited chatter filled the air. While Christina waited for the food to reach her, she counted nineteen kids in all. Only two of them were boys.

"Hey, Dylan," a girl with long, straight black hair called from the end of the table. "Catch." She threw a piece of broccoli at him.

"Ugh, no," Dylan said, crossing his arms over his head. He saw Christina watching and rolled his eyes before turning to grab the hot dog that Sean swiped from his plate.

In no time, Christina was stuffing herself with

potato chips and fooling around with the rest of the kids. All the girls were ganging up on Sean and Dylan and the insults were flying.

"What's with the long hair, Sean? Are you and Jester going to have matching braids?"

Sean smoothed the blond hair away from his face and struck a pose. "On your knees, peon. You are addressing the greatest Hamlet that ever graced the stage of John F. Kennedy Middle School."

Rachel, the girl who hit Dylan with the broccoli, sent a pickle through the air. Sean ducked just as Eliza came in. The pickle stuck to her shirt like a corsage.

Eliza looked down, making a big deal out of plucking off the pickle. Then she laughed and aimed it at Rachel, who swatted it in time to send it into the potato chips. "Move over," Eliza said, giving Rachel such a big push they both ended up in a laughing heap on the floor.

"Ms. Perkins says to pipe down," Dana said, standing with her hands on her hips in the doorway.

"Hey, pickle. Have a sour Dana," Sean said, his face perfectly straight. Christina almost choked on her milk.

"You mean, Sour. Have a Dana pickled," Melanie countered.

Dana glared as the table erupted in laughter. She turned without a word and disappeared into the other room where the instructors were eating.

When they finally got their breath back, Jennifer

whispered, "She's got an even better sense of humor this year."

After dinner, Ms. Perkins summoned everyone out on the front porch for ice-cream sandwiches and a meeting. Melanie, Jennifer, and Dylan got to the porch swing first.

"Hey, Christina. Come on," Dylan called, but Rachel got there before she did. "Sorry," Dylan mouthed. Christina made a "that's okay" face and found a spot on the railing. She hooked her feet around the spindles as she ran her tongue along the edge of her ice-cream sandwich and watched everyone move over to make more room in the swing. Rachel ended up half sitting in Dylan's lap.

Probably planned it that way, Christina thought. Dylan had to squirm sideways and put his arm across the back of the swing, but he didn't look like he minded. Honestly, couldn't he tell that Rachel was flirting with him? Then Sean went over to the swing and ended up lying across their legs.

Most of the kids were settled now, sprawled over the porch, steps, railings, and chairs. Eliza was talking and laughing with a couple of girls. If Christina hadn't seen firsthand how nasty Eliza could be, she would have thought she was someone she could be friends with.

The screen door squeaked when Ms. Perkins appeared with a clipboard in hand. A tall guy with glasses and a killer smile and a sandy-haired girl cuddling a fat calico cat followed. Dana and Adrianne brought up the rear.

When Ms. Perkins approached the swing, clearing her throat with a pointed, "Ahem," Dylan stood up and the rest followed. Sean rolled off, landing with a thump on the floor.

"I see you're practicing for tomorrow, Sean," Ms. Perkins said. "How fortunate to know how to roll in case you and Jester go separate ways."

Everyone laughed, including Sean. Ms. Perkins settled into the porch swing and waited while the kids got settled again. Christina hoped that Dylan would come over by her, but he sat down on the floor in front of Ms. Perkins.

"Let me begin by welcoming you to the twentieth annual Saddlebrook Event Camp. For those of you who are attending this clinic for the first time, I am Ms. Perkins, the camp director. My associate, Frieda Bruder, will be joining us a week late this year as she had to judge the FEI North American Championships in New England." Mrs. Bruder had been the judge at the small eventing show back home where Christina took lessons. Christina knew she could be tough.

Ms. Perkins paused as she looked around with the kind of smile that makes everyone smile back. "I feel privileged to have the opportunity to work each year with such a promising group of young riders."

Cheers began and Sean jumped up to take a quick bow before Dylan pulled him back down.

"And I do mean work," Ms. Perkins continued. "As usual, you have been divided into teams of four and assigned stalls next to each other." Ms. Perkins read down the list of names. Christina's team was Team Three. Sean, Dylan, Rachel, and Bekka, a thin girl with curly red hair, were in Team Five.

"In most cases," Ms. Perkins noted, "you have been assigned cabins together as well."

"Unless you're a boy and get the deluxe suite over the carriage house," Bekka shouted.

"It makes up for all the abuse we have to take," Sean said.

"You love every minute of it."

Ms. Perkins clapped her hands. "During these three weeks," she continued, "one of the things your teams will be judged on is stable management. It will be the job of our junior instructors, Dana Edwards and Adrianne Hillard, to take away points if anyone on your team has a dirty horse, stall, or tack."

Bekka raised her hand. "Since three out of the four horses on our team have white coats that get . . ." She paused for a second before continuing. "Er, *stained* easily, could we start out with a few extra points? You know, like a handicap?"

Naturally, Sean, Dylan, and Rachel chimed in that they thought it was a good idea, but everyone else booed.

"Nice try, Bekka," Ms. Perkins said. "But this is not golf. If Team Five needs some extra shampoo, however, I'm sure the tack shop next door has a good selection."

"Jody Adams and Nathan Hitchcock have joined us this year as instructors." Ms. Perkins made them stand up. "Both Jody and Nathan are on the United States Combined Training Association Young Riders team for our region, so we're very lucky to have them."

As Christina joined the applause, she hoped that someday she'd be standing in Jody's place.

"I know it's been a long day for everyone," Ms. Perkins said, "and I want you all in your cabins by nine o'clock, lights out at nine-thirty."

Nine-thirty. Christina hadn't gone to bed that early since fifth grade.

"You'll need to be at the barn by seven o'clock each morning to feed your horses and muck out their stalls. I'll let you know which riding group you've been assigned to when you come up for breakfast at eight o'clock. Horses must be tacked up and ready for lessons by nine o'clock."

"I feel like I've joined the Marines," Melanie griped as she, Christina, and Jennifer followed a group of kids down the driveway to check out the show jumps.

"You haven't seen anything yet," Jennifer said. "Perky's okay, but wait until Frieda gets here." She bent down, grabbing a handful of grass as she ran to catch up to the kids in front. "Right, Sean?" she said, trying to stuff it down the back of his shirt.

As Christina walked an imaginary course around the brightly painted jumps, she pretended that she and Sterling were flying over them in front of an admiring crowd. They were just approaching the brick wall when Rachel cut in front of her, running and screaming as she zigged to get away from Dylan, who was threatening to put a chunk of dried manure down her back. Jennifer and Melanie ambushed him from the side.

Christina couldn't believe Dylan was acting so immature. Probably because he couldn't go two steps without a girl falling all over him. It must be a pretty big ego trip to be one of the only boys at the camp. No way was she going to make a fool of herself trying to get his attention.

Besides, she was here to be a better rider. After having such a rough start, Christina was determined to prove to Dana and Eliza that she knew her stuff. Team Three was going to be the high-point winner if it killed her.

Jody and Nathan organized a game of capture the flag—A Barn against B Barn—on the lawn in front of the house. Christina's long legs put her at a definite advantage as she wove her way through the opposing team, rescuing her teammates from the jail. Once she'd even caught Dylan when he'd stolen their flag. By the time Ms. Perkins rang the warning bell for going back to the cabins, A Barn had won its second game.

"We're number one. We're number one," Melanie and Jennifer chanted as they put their arms around Christina and the other kids in A Barn, forming a wavy line across the field that finally collapsed in giggles on the grass. When they all started back to the kennel, Christina decided to take a detour through the barn so that she could say good night to Sterling.

Her mare was hanging over the stall door, nodding her head as Christina ducked under the rail. "You goof, what are you doing—wait a minute. What do you have in your mouth?" Sterling ducked back into the dim stall, but not before Christina saw what she'd done.

"Oh no," she said, rubbing the chewed part on Flash's rein. She jumped as Eliza grabbed it out of her hand.

"You should have told me Sterling chewed." Eliza's face was white with anger.

"I didn't know she did," Christina said, her heart still hammering from Eliza sneaking up on her like that. "At home we keep our stuff in a tack room."

Eliza frowned. "Well, I guess we don't have the setup *you* have. If your horse is the type that grabs things, you should have brought a stall guard to keep her head in."

"I'm sorry," Christina said, reaching for the rein. It was bumpy and bent in two places, but it wasn't damaged to the point that it would break. "I bet if I rubbed some Neatsfoot oil into it, you'd hardly be able to see where she chewed."

Eliza snatched the bridle back. "You've done enough damage already."

Who did she think she was? "Suit yourself," Christina said. "But you don't have to be so nasty about it. If you had put the bridle away in your tack trunk instead of letting it hang outside, Sterling wouldn't have been able to get at it in the first place."

"I'm not going to keep the bridle in my trunk," Eliza said. "It's not good for the leather to be shut up like that."

"And this was better?"

Eliza gave her a disgusted look and turned away.

"I'll go to the tack shop down the road and buy a stall guard tomorrow," Christina said as she turned to leave.

Christina heard Eliza mutter something about rich kids, but she kept walking. She was too tired to fight anymore.

4

"YOU ARE SO BAD," CHRISTINA SCOLDED STERLING THE
next morning. "If you had to chew, why didn't you
pick something inexpensive, like a lead line?" Her
voice wasn't angry though, because Sterling wouldn't
understand why she was mad. It was just nice to be
able to talk to Sterling, to get things off her chest. Eliza
wouldn't even look at her in the cabin this morning,
and Melanie and Jennifer weren't very good company, walking around half asleep.

Being with Sterling worked its usual magic, and by
the time the morning feeding was finished, Christina
was excited about their first lesson.

Breakfast was scrambled eggs and bacon, and
Dylan saved her a seat. His arm pressed against hers as
he asked, "How do you like it so far?"

"I like it," Christina said. "But I wish we could have

been on the same team. Eliza is getting on my nerves."

"Really?" Dylan said. "She always seemed okay to me. And she's a really good rider."

"Yeah? Well, Sterling got hold of Flash's bridle—" Christina was starting to tell him when Ms. Perkins came in.

"Good morning, everyone," she said, her singsongy voice ringing out over the talking. "I'm sure you're eager to hear your riding groups, which, as you may have gathered, are different from your teams."

Everyone quieted down in a hurry.

"The groups will be a little larger than usual until Frieda arrives next week, but Adrianne and Dana will be rotating around to assist us. Rachel, Anita, Melanie, Poe, Bekka, and Christina will be with Jody in the show ring. Dylan, Sean, Julie, Eliza, Sarah, Jessica, and Jennifer will be with me in the long dressage arena, and in Nathan's—"

Christina didn't even listen to the last group. There must be some mistake. She should be with Dylan, not Melanie.

As soon as Ms. Perkins finished, Christina jumped up to talk to her.

"Are these groups by level?" she asked.

Ms. Perkins looked over her half glasses at Christina. "We've tried to put students with similar experience together. Of course, with the six newcomers, I've had to take a guess based on the profile you sent with your application. Is there a problem?"

"I think so," Christina said. "You see, I've ridden a ton more than Melanie. I've already been in an event, and she's just starting."

"I see." Ms. Perkins took off her glasses. "Frieda Bruder helped prepare this list, and from what she said, your horse is still quite green."

"She is, but . . ."

"I find that it's best not to rush a young horse in its training," Ms. Perkins continued. "While I can understand your wanting to be in a more advanced group, you want to do what's best for your horse, don't you think?"

Christina nodded. When Ms. Perkins put it that way, how could she argue?

"And if we find that you are ready to move up during the course of the clinic, we will certainly not hold you back." Ms. Perkins smiled. "Now run along and tack up. You don't want to be late."

Christina grabbed her plate and glass and carried them into the kitchen. It wasn't fair to be put into a lower group just because Frieda happened to be the judge when Sterling was nervous and didn't do a terrific dressage test. Lots of horses were tense during shows. *When Jody sees how well Sterling goes for me today,* Christina thought, *she'll realize I'm in the wrong place.*

"Okay, you guys," Jody said, dragging a jump standard out of the way so that they would have more room. "Go

43

ahead and mount up. Just stay to the outside of the jumps as you walk around."

It felt to Christina as though Sterling was walking on tiptoes as they passed by the plywood boxes painted to look like a stone wall. "Silly girl. They won't bite you," Christina said, leaning forward to stroke her neck. Sterling felt her shift in weight and took it as a signal to trot. Christina let her, figuring that it would be good to let the mare work off a little of her nervous energy.

"Bring your horses over here," Jody said, motioning everyone to the cleared end of the ring. "At a *walk*, please."

As the kids straggled in, forming a circle around Jody, Christina noticed that Sterling was the tallest horse in the group.

"I see some new faces, so let's start by going around and introducing yourself and your horse. Rachel, why don't you start?"

Rachel was riding a dappled gray, too, but it was much smaller and rounder than Sterling. *Must be an Arabian*, Christina thought, noting its fine dished head.

"My name is Rachel and this is Nymph. Naughty Nymph is her show name."

Jody walked over and rubbed Nymph's nose. "Are you ready to go cross-country this year?"

Rachel's shoulders went up to her ears. "I guess," she said.

"You'll be fine." Jody smiled and tugged Rachel's ponytail, which came down to her waist.

"And you are . . ." Jody walked to Melanie.

"Melanie Graham."

"And who is this guy?" Jody said, patting Trib's brown-and-white neck. Trib blew through his nose at her.

"Tribulation," Melanie said. "Trib for short. Everyone says we're a perfect match."

Jody raised her eyebrows. "That bad, huh? What have you and Trib done together?"

Melanie scrunched up her face while she thought. "Well, he tries to buck me off a lot."

"Have you evented him?"

"Not yet." Melanie squared her shoulders. "But I'm game."

"I bet you are," Jody said, laughing.

A girl with braces introduced herself as Poe. Her horse was a bay—brown with a black mane and tail. Poe's legs could hardly fit around his barrel, he was so round.

"I see Pork Chop has fallen off his diet again," Jody said.

Poe laughed. "I know. I try to keep him in the paddock where there isn't much grass, but Mom always feels sorry for him and opens the gate into the field. You can look so pathetic," she said, leaning forward to pat Pork Chop's solid neck.

Anita was small, and with her big eyes and curly blond hair she looked closer to nine than twelve. Her pony, Mushroom, was the smallest in the camp.

45

"He could almost walk under Sterling's belly," Christina said.

Rachel shot her a look. "He might be short, but he can jump anything. Anita's in Pony Club with me."

Christina was taken aback at the way Rachel acted as if she thought Christina had insulted Mushroom. Eliza and Rachel were friends. Was Eliza going to turn Rachel against her, too?

Jody was fussing over Mushroom. "Haven't I seen you before?" she asked Anita.

"Were you at the Royalton Park Schooling Event this spring? I took him elementary, but we didn't place. We have to work on our dressage."

"I was a fence judge on cross-country. He went around that course like a rocket."

Anita nodded. "He went around the dressage ring that way, too."

"Then I guess you'll have your work cut out for you during this clinic." Jody smiled and turned to the next girl.

"Bekka. What happened to your new horse?"

Bekka's legs hung below the girth of the Appaloosa she was riding. "She got a gravel in one of her front hooves. Dad will bring her as soon as she's sound." She reached behind the saddle to give her pony a pat. "So it looks like it's Poko and me again."

Jody laughed. "Poor Poko. Just when she thought she was finished with jumping."

Now it was Christina's turn. "I'm Christina Reese and this is Sterling Dream."

Jody rested her hand on Sterling's neck as she sized her up. "How long has she been off the track?"

"She ran her last race in May." Christina hesitated before asking, "How could you tell?"

Jody ran her hand along Sterling's stomach. "See these muscles here? How tight and well developed they are? That's the sign of a horse that's been racing fit." She reached up behind Christina's saddle. "Now these muscles here and here," Jody moved to the top of Sterling's neck. "They aren't very well developed yet. I bet you have a hard time keeping her round and on the bit, don't you?"

Christina nodded. "Sometimes we get it and she feels like heaven under me. But a lot of the time she has her head up and goes too fast."

Jody smiled. "She has to learn a whole new way of carrying herself. It may take a while, but when she gets it she'll be nice."

Christina felt warm inside as if she were the one to have gotten the compliment. Jody sounded as though she knew a lot. Maybe this group wouldn't be so bad after all.

Jody clapped her hands. "Okay, everyone. Let's see your stuff. Spread out along the rail, and when you're ready, working trot, rising."

Melanie rode Trib next to Rachel's horse and just missed being kicked.

"You need to put a red ribbon on Nymph's tail to let riders know that she's a mare that doesn't like other horses getting too close," Jody warned.

Christina gathered her reins until she could feel Sterling's mouth. She guided her to a clear spot, then closed her legs onto her sides. Sterling leaped forward into a quick trot.

"Don't surprise her like that, Christina. Ride a half halt so you can balance her before you ask for a transition to trot. Do you know what a half halt is?"

Christina had to turn Sterling onto a fifteen-meter circle around a brush jump to try to slow her down. "Yes."

"Then close your legs and outside rein and sit as you quietly ask her to walk again."

Christina bounced four or five strides before Sterling gave in.

"That was a little too much hand and not enough leg," Jody said, motioning Christina over so that she could demonstrate. "When she's running around like that, she's leaning on your hands and her balance is way too far forward." Jody leaned forward and ran with her legs kicking out behind her. She looked like a clown who was trying not to fall.

"That's what Sterling is doing when she's trotting too fast. It was okay for her to be on her forehand like that when she was running down the track, but you'll need to teach her to shift her weight back to her hindquarters so you're not feeling like you're holding her up with your hands." Now Jody walked upright, with her shoulders held back. "When you can do that, her dressage will improve one hundred percent." Jody smiled. "Now try it again."

Christina chewed on the inside of her mouth as she brought Sterling out to the rail again. She closed her legs on Sterling as the mare leaped forward again.

"Sit up when you squeeze her. You should almost feel as though you are leaning backward. Ask her again."

Christina practiced a few more times before Jody turned away.

"You're getting it, Christina. A lot of walk-to-trot-to-walk transitions will really help this mare—if you remember your half halts."

Christina felt limp already and they had only just barely started the lesson. Three hours a day of this kind of intensive instruction and Sterling was bound to turn into the kind of event horse she wanted. She dropped her feet out of her stirrups and dangled them as she let Sterling take a breather. Boy, were her legs tired.

Christina's eyes wandered across the driveway to the dressage arena. Everyone was standing by the A marker while Ms. Perkins talked. As Christina watched, Eliza and Flash moved away from the group and picked up a trot. Flash looked gigantic as he lifted his back and moved down the side, his neck round and his tail carried high behind. Would Sterling ever move with such spring in her steps?

When Eliza turned at the H marker and headed down the diagonal, Flash's trot grew longer and longer as he skimmed across the sand. If Eliza had been wearing a black derby and a fancy dressage coat with tails, they'd look just like one of the German riders in the video on her bedroom shelf.

Christina groaned as she turned away. As horrible as it was to admit, Eliza was exactly the kind of rider Christina wanted to be.

"Ouch," Melanie said as she dismounted back at the barn. Christina knew just what she meant. When she had gotten off Sterling, the muscles along the insides of her legs had hollered, too.

When Jennifer took off her helmet, her bangs were plastered to her forehead. "You haven't seen anything yet. By the time this clinic is over, you'll have legs of steel." They laughed as she slapped her thigh because her leg was about as big around as a stick.

"Nice extended trot," Christina said as Eliza rode up. "Flash can really move."

"Thanks," Eliza said, swinging her leg over the saddle and landing lightly on the ground. "But it was really a lengthening." She ran her stirrup irons up on both sides, then reached for a halter.

Well, ex-cuuuuse me, Christina said to herself. Being friendly to Eliza was hopeless.

After Christina untacked Sterling, she practically

had to give her a sponge bath, the mare was so sweaty. As Christina ran the scraper along Sterling's hair to flick away the excess water, Dylan walked across the green with Dakota in tow.

"I'll show you a place by the river where we can cool these guys off," Dylan said.

"Just a sec," Christina said, remembering Jennifer's hat hair. She pulled out her elastic band and bent over, running her fingers along her scalp. When she straightened, she gathered the thick mass with one hand and wound the elastic back around it again. "Okay," she said, pulling the loose end of Sterling's lead line and giving her a little tug. "Let's go."

Finally she was going to have Dylan to herself for a few minutes. Maybe he'd have some ideas about Eliza.

He grinned at her as they walked side by side, and her stomach flip-flopped. "How was your lesson?"

"Great," Christina answered. "Jody's a really good teacher. She gave me some tricks to use when—"

"Hey, wait up you guys."

Christina tried to ignore the voice, but Dylan stopped. Rachel and Nymph were trotting side by side to catch up.

"Going to the stream?" Rachel asked, slightly out of breath.

Say no, Christina silently pleaded, but Dylan didn't pick up her telepathy. "Yeah. I figured it might be hot enough for even Sterling to go in the water. Want to come?"

"Sure," Rachel said. "If you all don't mind."

Christina minded, but what could she say?

Sterling hated water. She was only just now starting to walk into it without a fight, but Christina never knew when she could count on her. And since a lot of cross-country courses had water jumps, Sterling's dislike of water was a big deal.

The stream was shallow and inviting—at least to the other horses. Nymph practically dragged Rachel down the wide, gently sloping bank into the foot-deep water. Dakota followed, dropping his head to drink before wandering off the stony ford to a part that went up to his knees. Dylan perched on a rock at the edge, holding the lead line as the gelding started pawing and splashing water everywhere.

"He likes to get his stomach wet," Dylan explained, ducking as Dakota switched legs and sent cascades of water in their direction.

"See all the fun you're missing out on?" Christina tried to get Sterling to step in with the others, but the mare was content to watch, her toes on the very edge.

"Remember last year when we got to swim the horses in the Jacobs's pond?" Rachel said. "And Dana fell apart because she thought Fantasia was trying to buck her off in the water? Remember how . . ."

Rachel went on and on. It sounded as though she and Dylan had spent every second together last year at camp, to hear her talking. Finally Christina had had enough.

"I don't think we're going in today," she said, leading Sterling back up the bank.

"Maybe we can try again after our lesson this afternoon," Dylan said. "She might do better when you're riding and following another horse through."

"Will we get to go on a trail ride sometime?" Christina asked. The woods beyond the stream looked cool and inviting.

"Sure. We usually go out when it's too hot for a regular lesson," Rachel said. "Hey, Dylan. Remember the time when . . ."

As soon as Sterling was cool enough to go in her stall without breaking into a sweat again, Christina put her away.

"Sterling," Christina complained as the mare drank almost a full bucket of water. "Why didn't you drink at the stream? I don't appreciate having to fill your water bucket every time I turn around."

Melanie collapsed on her tack box, slumping against the barn wall as Christina tossed a cut of hay over the door for Sterling. "Do you want to come with me to the tack shop before lunch?" Christina asked. "I have to pick up a stall guard."

"No way," Melanie said, closing her eyes. "I'm going to just sit here and veg out."

Christina glanced around to see if anyone else was available. Eliza looked comfortable propped under a tree with a magazine while Flash grazed beside her. Maybe she'd be friendlier after the stall guard was in place.

The tack shop was supposedly just around the corner from Saddlebrook Farm, but by the time Christina had walked down the long driveway and a quarter of a mile up the road, ten minutes had passed. She sighed with pleasure as she stepped into the air-conditioned shop.

The woman behind the counter was knitting a sweater. How could anyone even touch wool in this weather?

"Stall guards are just past the brushes over on the left," the woman said, pointing with a knitting needle. "And the screw eyes for fastening them are down here, in front of the register."

Christina found what she needed right away. Since she wasn't ready to face the heat again just yet, she decided to browse around a little longer.

When she got to the bridles she paused, fingering the reins. Maybe she should buy a new pair for Eliza, to replace the ones Sterling messed up. She looked through the assortment of laced, linen, braided, and webbed reins until she found a pair like Eliza's— leather with strips of rubber on the part where the rider's hands go. They weren't cheap, but her mother owed her a few allowances.

She took the reins and stall guard up to the counter and on impulse added a poster of Olympic three-day eventer Mark Todd taking a dappled gray over a huge water jump. His horse reminded her of Sterling. Besides, it would brighten up the cabin.

"My parents opened an account for me to use while I'm at Saddlebrook," Christina said.

"Just sign here, honey," the lady said, pushing a slip of paper across the counter. "I'll put it on your tab."

The green was empty when Christina got back. She stuffed the bag with the reins and stall guard into her tack trunk and hurried to the big house for lunch.

After lunch, they broke into two groups for a lecture down at the barns. Dana was in charge of A Barn.

"Today we're going to talk about the *proper* way to groom a horse," she said. "Jennifer, will you get Fantasia out of her stall and bring her over?" Dana smiled at the group. "We'll use my horse for the demonstration."

"Right, Dana. Make *us* slave to get your horse clean," Jennifer joked as she got up.

Dana ignored the comment and went on. "And while Jennifer is getting Fantasia, why don't I go over the team point system."

Everyone got quiet while Dana flipped over a paper on her clipboard.

"You are graded in four areas each day with eight points being the highest you can get. Each person's points are added up to make the team's score. If all four people on a team get a perfect score, the team will have thirty-two points because four times eight equals thirty-two. Get it?" Dana looked around to make sure everyone was listening.

"I think we all know our times tables, Dana," Eliza said.

Dana pretended not to hear. "Area one: inside the stall. I'll be checking that your horse is clean, buckets are full, bedding is picked out, etc. If everything looks good, you get two points. If you have a dirty bucket or stall, you only get one point. If things are a real mess, you get a warning instead of points."

"So if my horse has to pee I lose a point?" Melanie said. "What am I supposed to do? Use Pampers?"

Dana scowled. "I can tell if the stall was clean and dry before dinner. Area two," she continued. "Tack and tack trunk. You're expected to leave your saddle and bridle clean and neatly put away each day."

"Watch out for sweat marks. They really look for those," Eliza whispered.

"Area three: the barn itself. The aisle in front of the stalls must be raked and all tools must be neatly tied up." Dana looked at Christina when she said this.

"Area four: miscellaneous. If you break any other rules like, say, being noisy during lectures, you'll lose points. Any questions?"

Melanie raised her hand. "You forgot something."

"What?" Dana said, looking back at her clipboard with a worried expression.

"You forgot to say, 'Welcome to the army.'"

This time, Dana raised her voice over the laughter. "We didn't count the first night, but if we had, some of you know-it-alls would have lost points for your team." Dana looked right at Melanie. "You would have lost a point for your tack trunk. It's a mess." She continued reading down the list. "Christina would have lost two points. One for tying her horse improperly and one for not having enough water in her stall."

"But I filled Sterling's bucket to the brim at dinner," Christina protested.

"If your horse drinks a lot of water, you need to hang up a second bucket."

Christina burned as Dana read on. Every single one of them would have lost at least one point if last night had counted. Even Eliza. She bet Adrianne wasn't so picky.

The grooming demonstration was pretty boring, too. Dana mostly asked for volunteers, then told everyone what they were doing wrong. And it was stuff Christina already knew, anyway.

She watched Eliza pull out a plastic bag with lots of different colors of embroidery floss. She pinned a partially braided piece to the leg of her breeches, then started to work. Christina enjoyed watching the braid grow longer as Eliza's fingers deftly picked at the strands. Christina had never seen that type of rolled braid before.

"Cool. Are you making those again? I lost the one I bought from you last year and I haven't found another one I like as much," Jennifer whispered as she scooted over to watch. "How much?"

"Three dollars. Same as last year."

"Will you do mine next? I'll pick out the colors." Jennifer grabbed the bag.

"That's a bargain. They cost twice that in New York," Melanie said, pulling floss out of the bag, too.

By the time Dana put Fantasia away, Eliza had so many orders for the bracelets that she had to get a pen from her tack trunk to write them all down. Even Christina decided to order two identical ones for herself and Katie.

When the crowd had cleared from around Flash's stall as kids drifted away to get ready for the afternoon lesson, Christina remembered the reins.

"I bought these to replace the ones Sterling damaged," she said, pulling the new stiff reins out of the bag and handing them to Eliza.

Eliza ran her thumb along the expensive leather. "You didn't have to do that."

It was the closest Eliza had come to sounding halfway decent. "I wanted to. I also bought this," Christina said, reaching in for the stall guard. "Do you like Mark Todd?"

Eliza shrugged. "Who wouldn't?"

"Ta da," Christina said, pulling the last thing out of the bag. "I got a poster of him for our cabin."

"Must be nice to be able to buy anything you want," Eliza said, turning away.

Christina felt as though she'd been slapped in the face. "What is your problem?" she said, catching Eliza's arm.

Eliza looked down at Christina's hand before lifting it off like it was a piece of dirty laundry. "I don't think *I'm* the one with the problem around here."

"Yeah? Well, I think you have a problem if you can't even see that I'm trying to make up for what Sterling did."

"Come on, Cuz," Melanie said. "She's being a jerk."

As Christina allowed herself to be pulled away, she wondered why on earth Eliza hated her so much.

5

CHRISTINA DIDN'T ENJOY THE AFTERNOON LESSON VERY much. She couldn't shake off the unpleasant feeling that was left from her fight with Eliza.

After they warmed up and trotted and cantered over some fifteen-inch cavalletti, Jody set up three jumps in a row that she called gymnastics.

"Okay, Melanie. Why don't you go first?"

Melanie looked a little apprehensive as Trib trotted toward the first jump. He popped over it, took a canter stride, and jumped the second fence so big that Melanie was left leaning back in the saddle like the riders in old-fashioned hunt prints. The third jump was better, but when Trib's feet touched the ground he put down his head and gave a playful buck.

"Whoa," Melanie said, laughing as she leaned back rodeo style. Christina had to admit that even though Melanie's position wasn't always the best, she made up for it in guts. Her cousin didn't let Trib intimidate her with his pony tricks.

After they had gone through the gymnastics a few more times, Jody turned to the group. "Okay, Christina. Let's see you next."

As Christina picked up a trot, her heart beat like it did at a show. With everyone watching, she wanted to do it right the first time.

Sterling's ears went forward and back as they turned the corner and faced the gymnastics. From this angle, it was hard to tell where one jump ended and the next one began.

Sterling broke into a canter a few strides in front of the jumps, so Christina circled her away. They were supposed to trot into the first fence.

She managed to keep Sterling in a trot the second try, but the mare's ears were pinned back in displeasure, her hindquarters swishing from side to side as they approached the jumps. Sterling exploded over the first fence, jumping it twice as big as she needed. This brought her so close to the second fence that she had to twist in the air to clear it. Her jump over the third fence, more of a square than a smooth, easy arc, almost unseated Christina.

"Okay," Jody called as Christina's foot groped for her outside stirrup. The toe of her boot had slipped out during Sterling's last awkward jump. "This time, establish a good forward trot *before* you turn Sterling down the long side toward the jumps. When you grab her mouth to slow her down in front of the fence, she jumps flat. You need to *allow* her to use her back."

"If I don't use my hands, she'll go through them too fast," Christina said.

"That's why these gymnastics will help," Jody explained. "Since the jumps are set up so she only has room for one short canter stride between them, they'll force her to shift her weight and balance back to her hind legs and take her time going through them. You may have a few more awkward runs, but she'll figure out the most comfortable way to handle the jumps as long as you're not setting up a tug-of-war and distracting her."

Christina tried to do what Jody said, but Sterling always surged ahead as soon as she was pointed toward the jumps and Christina couldn't keep from pulling back on the reins.

"Give her a breather now," Jody said, shaking her head as she fixed the two poles Sterling had knocked off the standards during their last headlong rush. "You two are still fighting each other," she continued, walking back to the group. "You have to let the gymnastics slow her down." Jody must have seen the tears welling up in Christina's eyes. Her voice softened. "Don't worry. You'll get it," she said, touching Christina's boot before turning to the next rider. "Okay, Rachel. Let's see if Nymph remembers this stuff."

It was too hot to be riding, and Christina had a

headache where her helmet pressed into her forehead. Fortunately, Jody finished up by having them jump a little course. Sterling was a lot quieter jumping the individual fences and Christina felt pretty good until she rode back to the group.

"We'll need to work on Sterling's form," Jody said. "She's not using herself properly. It's not a big deal over small jumps like these, but if you want to go training level or higher, you'll have to help her learn to use her back better."

Christina hung behind the others on the way back to the barn. She felt like such a failure. Maybe she wasn't a good enough rider to train Sterling after all.

It seemed as though Eliza was going out of her way to talk to everyone but Christina during evening chores. Even Melanie seemed to have forgotten how awful Eliza had acted to Christina. They were giggling as Eliza took over from Jennifer in trying to help Melanie pull off her stuck boot. Eliza's back was to Melanie as she held the boot between her legs like a blacksmith. Melanie was getting jerked forward with each yank, so she planted her other foot on Eliza's backside to keep from sliding off the tack trunk. When the boot finally came off, Eliza pitched forward with a shriek of laughter.

So why was Eliza being nice to Melanie? Was Christina the only person in the place she didn't like?

Christina was one of the first ones to finish up in the barn for a change. She went straight to the cabin instead of hanging around with the others, glad for a chance to have some time by herself.

After dinner, everyone walked to the high school down the road where the town's Founders Day carnival and fireworks were being held. Christina had been looking forward to the rides and games, but now she would rather have just crawled into bed. Her arms ached from Sterling pulling on them, and she was tired of smiling and pretending everything was okay.

"Come on," Melanie said as she tried to hurry Christina along so that they could catch up with the rest of the group. "I can smell the cotton candy."

"The way my luck's going, it'll probably end up in my hair," Christina said.

"What's the matter?"

"I don't know," Christina said. "Camp's not turning out the way I expected."

"Why? Don't you think Jody's a good teacher?"

"Yeah," Christina said, slowing even more. "I just wish Eliza wasn't on our team."

"She's not so bad, really," Melanie said. "You guys just started off on the wrong foot. I think you have to give her time to cool down."

"But *I* didn't do anything," Christina said, stopping in the road.

Melanie sighed. "Look. Sometimes you just have to roll with the punches. If you let Eliza get to you, you won't have anyone to hang out with."

Traitor, Christina thought.

"Want me to tell them you're sick?" Melanie offered. "Of course, they'll probably send Dana back to the camp with you."

Nothing could be as bad as hanging out with Dana. Not even Eliza. "Okay, okay. You've convinced me," Christina said, smiling at Melanie's wicked grin.

"Beat you," Melanie said, starting to run.

Christina sprinted ahead. "In your dreams."

"Are you going on the Ferris wheel?" Melanie asked Jennifer when they crossed the school parking lot toward the athletic field. The rides of the small carnival twinkled in the evening light.

"No way. I'm afraid of heights."

"That little thing," Sean said. "You jumped higher than that when Geronimo helicoptered you over the stone wall this afternoon."

Everyone laughed, even Christina.

"I hate it when horses do that," Eliza said. "When Flash jumps a Liverpool, I swear he's clearing it with three feet to spare."

"You should have seen Sterling over the gymnastics today," Christina said. "She almost jumped out from under me."

Eliza glanced Christina's way, then turned her back and started talking to Jennifer.

Christina stopped in her tracks, but Dylan and the others didn't even notice she had dropped behind. *Who cares*, she told herself, deciding to go on her own to explore the different stands.

There was a place to fill bottles with layers of colored sand. Christina watched two little girls in matching sundresses make theirs. The older one was helping the younger girl pour her sand in. Christina wondered what it would have been like to have had an older sister. Would she have known how to deal with people like Eliza?

The next place had a glass case filled with quarters. Christina tried rolling her quarter down the shoot, hoping that it would be the one to push the rest off the ledge so that she could win. She used up ten quarters, only winning once and getting back three, before she moved on.

Even the caramel corn tasted flat to her. She just wasn't in the mood to have fun.

"Where have you been?" Melanie said, grabbing Christina from behind. Eliza, Rachel, Melanie, and Dylan were wearing plastic rings on their heads that glowed in the dark. Sean and Jennifer were dueling with plastic swords. "Come on. We're going to get a good spot for watching the fireworks."

Christina hadn't noticed how dark it was getting. The full moon stood out like a white ball in the blue-black sky. She let Melanie drag her to the side of a hill above the soccer field where volunteer firefighters were bustling around, getting ready to set off the firecrackers. It was mostly teenagers who perched around them. Families with little kids had chosen flatter ground to spread their blankets.

Sean rolled down the hill, pretending to be mortally wounded while Jennifer waved her blue sword and declared herself the winner. Dylan was deep in conversation with Rachel, describing the big Rolex event he had gone to watch. She looked like an exotic princess with her long hair spilling across her shoulders and the glowing green circle sitting like a crown on her head. Christina sat down to listen, too, even though she had heard it all before.

Melanie, Jennifer, and Eliza sat in front of them, partway down the hill. They were laughing as they fended off the grass that Sean was launching toward them using his sword as a catapult.

Maybe I am coming down with something, Christina thought as she sat there, out of it. She didn't feel any better when the fireworks started up. If anything, she felt worse because of the noise.

"I've got a headache," she told Dylan. "Tell Melanie I'm going back to the cabin."

"Okay," Dylan said, smiling at her before the next explosion caught his attention. He stuck his fingers in his mouth and whistled. "All right!"

"Excuse me. Excuse me," Christina said as she picked her way through the spectators.

"Where are you going?" Dana said, her hand reaching out to grab Christina's leg.

"To the bathroom," Christina said, shaking her off. If she told her the truth, Dana would probably make her stay.

She got away from the crowd without anyone else stopping her. Ms. Perkins even waved before turning to say something to the woman beside her.

Just in case Ms. Perkins was watching, Christina headed toward the blue Porta Potties at the edge of the parking lot, but she ducked around back and kept on walking past the police car and the firefighters who were in charge of parking.

Her head felt better away from the noise and confusion. As her sneakers slapped the empty pavement, she realized practically everyone in town must be at the high school.

By the time she turned onto the gravel driveway of Saddlebrook Farm, she had made up her mind to call home—just to check in, of course. She didn't want her mother or father to know how homesick she was, or they might do something embarrassing like show up before Parents' Day on Sunday. But it would feel good to hear their voices.

There was only one light on in the house and Christina knew before she even set foot on the porch that the woman who cooked for them had probably locked the door behind her when she left. She was right. As the knob refused to turn in her hand, she felt an urge to kick the door. Instead, she headed to the barn to talk to Sterling.

The light on the flagpole cast a yellow glow along the neatly raked aisle. Christina hoped that Gus, the groundskeeper, wasn't around.

Shadowy figures moved in the stalls as she walked by. Pork Chop stuck out his head and nickered, so Christina stopped to say hello. His ears pricked forward as one of the fireworks broke above the trees next to the hay barn. Further down, she could hear a horse kick the side of a stall.

"It's okay," Christina said, her voice breaking the sleepy stillness of the barn. "Those are just fireworks. They won't hurt you."

The kicking continued, so Christina picked up her pace. She hoped it wasn't Sterling. Dana would probably find a way to blame it on her if Sterling broke a board in her stall.

Shoot, it is, Christina thought as she got to her stall. But Sterling met her at the door, her ears relaxed as Christina stretched up to scratch behind them.

She could feel the vibration from the next kick through her arm as she leaned on the door. "Flash? What's the matter, buddy?"

At first when she looked over Flash's door, she thought the stall was empty. The next kick directed her eyes downward, where she could just make out his large, dark form thrashing against the wall.

Christina's first instinct was to go in the stall and see what was wrong, but as her hand touched the latch and Flash kicked again, she had second thoughts. *If only it weren't so dark.* She racked her brain, trying to think if she had noticed any lights in the barn. But even if there were, she didn't know where to find the switch.

Wait a minute. Didn't she stick her Maglite in the tack trunk? She lifted out the top tray and felt around until her fingers closed on the slim flashlight. When she turned it on, the light poured out in a welcoming triangle that jiggled up and down as she turned back to Flash's door.

Flash was lying down. He looked huge stretched out in the stall, his head by the front wall and his legs almost touching the wall between him and Sterling.

Something was wrong, though. Flash raised his head as if he were going to stand, but his front legs struck the boards before he could pull himself up. He started thrashing around on the ground, his eyes rolling. Now Christina knew what was wrong. Flash couldn't get up.

6

"IT'S OKAY, BOY," CHRISTINA SAID, TRYING TO REASSURE him. She began trembling as the horse looked at her with desperate eyes. Flash must have been rolling on his back and accidentally flipped over so that he was left facing the wall. What should she do? How could she get him to a standing position all by herself?

The big horse was already panicking because he was trapped. Christina knew Flash could shatter a bone if he kept kicking out, or break a blood vessel in his brain if he kept struggling to stand up. Flash needed help quickly.

Christina looked toward the tractor shed where Gus hung out, but there wasn't any light on in his room. As Flash grunted and tried to get up again, Christina watched helplessly from the door. She had to try *something*.

Maybe she could flip him back over by herself. She'd seen the grooms do it at home a couple of times. She made up her mind. She had to try.

She dug through her trunk again to find her twenty-five-foot lunge line to put around Flash's legs. If she wrapped her end around the post at the door, she bet there would be enough leverage.

Christina opened the stall door all the way so that she could make a quick escape if necessary. She took a second to balance the flashlight on a ledge so that she'd have both hands free.

"Easy boy," Christina said, more than a little nervous about getting so close to those powerful legs. "I want to help." She unhooked the water bucket and set it outside the stall so that she'd have more room to work. When she came back in, Flash raised his head and tried getting up one more time. He kicked and thrashed and Christina could see the band of white around his eye as he struggled. His sides were heaving from trying so hard. She waited until he was still, his head back on the floor, before she moved.

Christina inched toward his head, pressing close to the front wall so that if he did manage to flip back over on his own, she wouldn't be crushed under his body. "Easy. Easy, buddy," she murmured as she made a loop with the lunge line and squatted down.

"What a good boy you are," she cooed, stroking his sweaty neck. "I'm just going to lean over you like this—" She took a deep breath and reached toward his front legs. "And loop this rope around like so—" Christina ran her hand down his leg and managed to hook the lunge line under both ankles. "And now I'm going to see if I can help pull you back over."

She slowly straightened and backed toward the door, her fists tight on the ends of the lunge line. "I hope this works," she said as she looped both pieces around the post and pulled.

Flash's front legs came up about a foot before the lunge line slid further up his leg and his hooves dropped back to the ground. "Oh no," Christina muttered, afraid the line might cut into his knees.

"Let's try that again," she said, putting her whole weight into it this time. The line moved up even further and Christina could see it wasn't going to work.

"Okay. Time out. We need to get this thing set up again." When Christina walked over to shift the lunge line back down his legs, she noticed a flat place in the sawdust.

"Hey. I think I dragged you out a little," Christina said. "I must be stronger than I thought."

Flash tried to get up again. For a second, Christina thought he might make it, but he still didn't have enough room.

"Okay. On the count of three, I want you to get up. One—" she oomphed. "Two—" Did he move out a little further? "Three." Christina leaned her full weight across the line. All of a sudden, the tension went slack and she was flat on her stomach in the dirty sawdust.

She instinctively rolled out of the way and jumped up at the same time Flash scrambled to his feet.

"We did it," she said, adrenaline pumping through her body. "All right, Flash!"

Flash shook like a dog, then stuck his nose down to sniff the place where he had lain, trapped. Christina was elated as she returned the water bucket to its hook and slipped outside. No telling what might have happened to Flash if she hadn't come along. And while she knew that the most important thing was that Flash was all right, she couldn't help but look forward to telling Eliza about the rescue.

Christina leaned over the door, watching as Flash circled the stall. He looked nervous, like he was checking to make sure everything was all right.

"You're okay, now. Eat your hay," Christina said.

Flash bit at his side as if he were going after a horsefly, then started to paw. Christina's mouth dropped open when she realized he was going to roll again.

"No," she shouted. Flash jerked up his head and looked at her for a second before lowering his nose and pawing.

"Don't roll!" This time Flash ignored her. He kicked out behind and smacked the side of the stall with his hooves before sniffing the sawdust again.

"Flash, come on. What's the matter with you? Please don't roll again. I don't think I could get you up this time." Flash didn't roll, but he continued to paw at the hay, bite at his side, and breathe heavily.

Then it hit her. Flash had a terrible stomachache. That's why he kept looking back at his side and biting at it. He was colicking. Colic killed more horses than any other sickness.

"No," Christina shouted again, startling him into staying on his feet. She grabbed the lead line hanging on the door and burst into the stall before he could turn his hindquarters to keep her away. She had to get him moving. Walking was the only way to keep him from rolling and possibly twisting his intestines. Flash needed a vet right away.

"Help," Christina yelled as she tried to get Flash to leave his stall. He almost pulled the lead rope out of Christina's hand. Finally she was forced to run the chain end through a ring in his halter and across his nose where it would apply pressure and hurt if he pulled back. Thank goodness that worked.

As she led Flash down the aisle of the barn, Christina kept calling for Gus. If Gus wasn't around and the house was locked so that she couldn't call anyone, what could she do? She wished she could remember if there had been a pay phone along the road by the tack shop.

Flash wasn't as hard to handle once she got him walking. Aside from jerking around every so often, biting and kicking at his belly, he went along willingly enough—until they got to the end of the barn. Christina tried to keep him going, but he planted his feet and wouldn't walk any further.

When a horse whinnied and Flash answered, nervously swishing his tail, she got an idea. "I know you don't want to leave your buddies, Flash, but we've got to get you some help. How about if I pony you?" Like all racehorses, he was probably used to being ponied—led by a groom on a quiet horse—whenever he went to the starting gate for a race. Maybe she could pony him to the road and flag down a car.

Should she take Sterling? Christina vetoed that idea right away. As much as she loved her mare, Trib would be a better choice. She didn't fancy trying to control two Thoroughbreds on the road.

Christina didn't dare risk tying Flash to the rail while she got Trib ready, even though it was awkward rummaging through Melanie's tack trunk for a bridle while trying to keep Flash's head up. Fortunately Trib came to the door, his ears pricked forward as he and Flash sniffed noses.

"Now I don't want any nonsense out of you two," Christina said, ready for the squeal or kick that often accompanied a first meeting. But Flash was more concerned about his stomach than showing Trib who was boss, and he stomped his back foot and swished his tail.

It wasn't any trouble putting Trib's bridle on in the shadowy doorway. She'd done it so many times, she could probably do it in her sleep. "Okay, Trib. I'm counting on you," Christina said, leading the pony out of the stall and hoping Flash wouldn't do anything crazy while she was sandwiched between them.

As soon as they got to the grass, Flash dropped his head, looking for a place to roll. Christina took the lead rope and reins in one hand and swung herself up onto Trib's broad, familiar back. It was easier to get Flash's head up again from this angle, and she used her legs to maneuver Trib so that Flash was on her right.

"Okay, Trib. It's up to us now," Christina said, squeezing him forward.

With Trib for company, Flash went willingly. Too willingly. Christina had a hard time keeping him from getting ahead as she tried to manage both reins in her left hand and Flash's lead line in the right.

When they got to the driveway, Flash lurched forward, almost pulling Christina from Trib's slippery back. "Whoa," she said firmly, pushing herself back from Trib's neck. She added a handful of mane to the reins in her hand to anchor herself better. Beside her, Flash grunted and bucked.

Maybe she was crazy to ride for help. But Flash was getting worse. What else could she do?

They somehow made it to the road. Christina stopped beside the lantern posts that stood on either side of the driveway, trying to decide which way to go. There was a glow of light to the left, in the direction of the high school. She couldn't see any fireworks, but occasional crackles and bangs told her they were still going on. Trib's head was up as though he were wondering what was making the noise, but his muscles stayed relaxed under her legs.

The road to the right seemed darker and more remote. "Come on, Trib," Christina said, neck-reining the pony to the left. She wanted to go where people were. The fireworks would probably be over any minute now, anyway, and she could flag down a car.

It was scary riding along with only the moonlight to guide them. The flashlight was in her pocket because it was too hard to manage with everything else she had to hold. She would grab it if a car came along.

They got to the top of the hill overlooking the high school just as the sky in front of them exploded with colors and whistles. Trib reeled around, sending Christina flying off his back and into the dark.

"Whoa," she shouted as her hip hit the ground, sending a jolt through her entire body. The horses' legs scrambled around her and she cradled her head and closed her eyes, bracing herself for the crash of an iron shoe against her helmet. Then the lead line tightened and she was jerked forward, her jeans making a rasping sound as Flash dragged her along the pavement.

Christina opened her hand to let go, but she still slid along the blacktop, the lights from the parking lot bouncing in the sky and her arm stretching so much she was afraid it was being torn in two. *It's wrapped around my wrist,* she thought, twisting against the line with all her strength. The pulling stopped and Christina went tumbling into the weeds.

7

IT TOOK A FEW SECONDS BEFORE HER HEAD QUIT SPIN-
ning enough so that she could get up. When she did,
the road in front of her was bright with flashing
lights.

Cars. Trib and Flash were loose on the road.

"Trib. Flash," she called, praying she wouldn't
hear a screech of brakes or—she shut her mind
against that other sound. She started running, surprised that her legs would still obey, and headed
toward the flashing lights from the police car that was
positioned at the school entrance to direct traffic.

"Tri-ib, Flash." She tried to pucker her lips for a
whistle, but her mouth was trembling too much. She
had to find the horses before they got hurt. As she
turned into the school driveway, she could hear a
voice shouting.

"We got 'em!"

Christina let out a giant sigh as a woman in a uniform walked across the parking lot leading Trib. Flash was still loose but following closely behind.

"Thank you," Christina said, her voice teary with relief as she hobbled up. "Easy, Flash."

The Thoroughbred's head hung down and he didn't resist when Christina took hold of the dangling lead line. She turned to the policewoman.

"This horse is sick. He needs a vet."

"Doc Harding is here. I'll go find him," a volunteer firefighter with an orange vest said. He sprinted toward the field.

"You better move those horses over there," another firefighter directed. "The fireworks are finished and cars are going to start coming out."

As Christina followed the policewoman over to the lighted grass cul-de-sac in front of the high school entrance, Melanie and Dylan ran up beside her.

"What happened?" Dylan said, his face full of concern. Melanie took Trib from the policewoman and turned back to Christina. Her mouth dropped open. "Look at your leg."

Christina was surprised at all the blood. "I got dragged," she said, wincing at the shredded denim of her favorite jeans.

At that moment, Rachel and Eliza ran up. Eliza's eyes were blazing.

"What have you *done* to him?" she shouted, wrenching the lead line out of Christina's hands. "You had no business taking him out of the stall."

This was the last straw. "For your information," Christina said, "your horse is sick. I was only trying to get him help."

Eliza turned to Rachel. "See what I mean? She thinks she can do whatever she wants."

"Will you just shut up and listen?" Christina felt like shaking Eliza. "Look at him. Can't you tell he's in pain?"

"Oh my gosh," Eliza said, taking a closer look at Flash. "Has he been rolling?"

"He was on the floor of the stall when I found him," Christina said. "But I kept him moving."

"Why didn't you call a vet?" Eliza's eyes were narrow as if it were all Christina's fault.

"Lighten up," Dylan said. "You're lucky Christina knew to keep him walking."

"I would have called, but the house was locked." Christina hated how defensive she sounded. "Somebody's getting the vet now."

"You'd better keep him walking," Rachel reminded Eliza.

"Boy. Flash did a number on your leg." Dylan took her arm. "Why don't you sit down before you bleed to death? I'll find Ms. Perkins."

"I'll help," Rachel offered. "She was just back by the crafts."

Dylan helped Christina to the stone wall around

the flagpole. She would have enjoyed his arm around her more if her leg hadn't started burning where the skin was scraped.

"Sit tight. I'll be right back."

With Dylan looking so concerned as he left, the enormity of what could have happened swept over Christina like a cold wave. What if she had broken her leg when she'd fallen? What if she hadn't been able to get her arm loose from the rope? Or worst of all, what if one of the horses had gotten hit by a car? Christina closed her eyes.

"You okay?" Melanie said as she sat down beside her. Trib nibbled grass around their feet.

Christina nodded as she brushed her eyes with her hand. Her palm was stinging, too.

Melanie cocked her head. "So how did you know Flash was sick?"

Christina took a deep breath and told her the whole story. She said it loud enough so that Eliza could hear as she walked Flash in a small circle around them.

"Where was Gus?" Eliza asked.

"I looked for him. He wasn't around."

A Toyota Land Cruiser drove toward them, stopping just at the edge of the grass. Ms. Perkins jumped out of the passenger side and a tall, thin man ducked out from the other side.

"What have we here?" Ms. Perkins said as she strode toward them as though she were still wearing boots. "Someone said you had a fall, Christina. Are you all right?"

"I am, but Flash isn't," Christina said. "I'm pretty sure he's colicking."

"Hmm," Ms. Perkins said, glancing over to where the vet was talking to Eliza. "Doc Harding will take care of him, but let's have a look at that leg. Can you stand?"

After Ms. Perkins was satisfied that Christina wasn't too seriously injured, they listened to the vet.

"I've given him a shot of Banamine for the pain," Doc Harding explained, lifting Flash's upper lip and looking at his gums. "His color's not too bad. The gums would be whiter if he were going into shock." The vet stuck his stethoscope into Flash's ears and worked his way back, gently resting his hand on Flash's barrel as he moved the metal disk from one spot to another. Christina held her breath as he turned.

"I can hear a lot of movement going on in his intestines, so I'm hoping we're looking at a gas colic." He looked at Christina. "You're the one who found him?"

"Yes. He was cast in his stall, but when I got him up, he started to roll again."

"And you got him up all by yourself?"

Christina nodded. "I used the post for a pulley."

Doc raised his eyebrows. "Well done, young lady. You might have saved this horse's life." He turned to Ms. Perkins. "Let's get him back to the farm so I can give him a complete going over."

Ms. Perkins stayed with Eliza and Melanie. "We'll head back with the horses as soon as the traffic has cleared," she said, sending Christina along with the vet.

Christina winced as she climbed into Doc's truck. It wasn't going to be fun taking the jeans off over her sore leg. "Do you think Flash will be okay?" she asked as they pulled into the line of cars waiting to leave the high school.

Doc's voice was reassuring. "It sounds like you found him before he did himself any real damage. But I can't make any promises yet. We'll have to see how it goes."

When Ms. Perkins came back, she sent everyone but Christina and Eliza to their cabins.

"Not fair," Melanie complained.

"Go," Ms. Perkins said in her no-nonsense voice.

Christina avoided looking at Eliza while Doc continued examining Flash.

"I don't feel any evidence that he's twisted his bowel," Doc said finally as he peeled off his long plastic glove. "And it's too soon to tell if there's a blockage."

"What kind of blockage?" Eliza asked.

"Food, most likely. Sometimes grain or hay will get backed up or impacted in the intestines. If that's the case, the shot I gave him will help him to relax so it may pass through on its own."

"And if it doesn't?" Eliza asked.

"Then I might have to tube him—run a tube through his nose into his stomach so I can pour mineral oil in to help move things along."

Christina liked the way he talked to them like adults.

Doc gave Flash one last pat before turning to Ms. Perkins. "Let him rest in his stall forty-five minutes. Then the rest of the night, walk him fifteen minutes out of every hour. If he starts kicking and showing a lot of pain again, give me a call and I'll come right away. Otherwise, I'll be back to check on him first thing in the morning."

Eliza watched Doc gather his instruments. "But what if he tries to roll again?"

"He shouldn't with the painkiller," Doc said. "But, of course, someone needs to stay with him to make sure."

"If he goes to the bathroom, will that mean he's going to be okay?" Christina asked.

Doc smiled. "It'll be a good sign."

"But what if he doesn't?" Eliza said, following Doc to the truck.

Doc ran his hand along his chin and sighed. "Then we may have to consider hospitalizing him."

"For an operation?" Christina knew that operating on horses was tricky. They could easily go into shock and die.

"Doesn't that cost a lot of money?" Eliza's face looked pinched and white under the floodlight.

Doc nodded, then said, "Let's not borrow trouble, Eliza. More often than not, colic responds to the treatment we're using."

Flash looked as if he had aged twenty years as he stood quietly at the rail, his eyes sunken and dull. He was really feeling out of it, poor guy. Christina crossed her fingers behind her back. She hoped Doc was right. She didn't like Eliza much, but she didn't have anything against her horse.

It was almost midnight before Ms. Perkins put down the peroxide and antibiotic cream and decided Christina's leg was clean and safe from germs. Christina had taken a bath in the big house so that her leg could soak in the water. It had taken her ten minutes to work up the nerve to get it wet. There were patches where the skin was rubbed raw from the outside of her knee to her ankle.

"Are you sure you don't want me to bandage it?" Ms. Perkins asked.

Christina considered the damage. Now that the bleeding had stopped, there wasn't too much to see. Just a lot of light pink patches that would be ugly and brown soon enough. "No. I hate pulling them off."

Ms. Perkins gently eased the leg of the sweatpants she'd loaned to Christina over the scrapes. "That should do you, then. Run along to bed. You've had a long day."

"What about Flash?"

"Eliza and Dana are taking the first shift. Adrianne and I will set our alarms for three o'clock and do the second shift." Ms. Perkins paused. "You did a fine job tonight."

"Thanks," Christina said. "I wish Eliza thought so, too."

Ms. Perkins sighed. "Eliza's upset, understandably so. It's too bad she's having such a rough summer."

Christina was just about to ask what she meant when Ms. Perkins yawned and looked at her watch. "Heavens, we need to get to bed. Now, scoot!"

Christina hesitated on the porch to see if they were walking Flash. The aisle lights were on in A Barn, but no one was in sight. *Just one quick peep before I go to bed*, she told herself as she headed down the walk.

The horses were quiet, most just lifting their heads and watching from their shadowy stalls as she made her way down the aisle. "Hello, pretty girl," Christina said when Sterling hung her head over the door and watched her approach. "You're not getting much sleep, either, are you?" She rubbed her mare behind the ears before moving to the next door. "Eliza?"

There was a short silence before the girl answered. "Yeah?"

Christina ignored the unfriendly tone. "How's Flash doing? Any change yet?" she said, peering into the dim stall. Flash stood in the center, his head still hanging. She couldn't see Eliza very clearly in the corner.

"No."

"But he's not trying to roll anymore, is he?" Flash didn't look as if he were in the mood to do anything.

"No."

Was Eliza crying? Her voice sounded thick. Christina looked around. "Where's Dana?"

"In bed. I wanted to be by myself."

Christina could take a hint. "Do you need anything before I go? A soda or something? I think Melanie still has some."

Eliza sniffed. "Sure."

"Okay," Christina said, surprised. "I'll go get one." For the second time that night, she rummaged through the black trunk.

Trib's bit was caked with dried grass. Maybe she'd better clean it since it was sort of her fault it had gotten dirty. She didn't want to give Dana an excuse to dock any points from their team.

Christina tossed the bridle over to her tack trunk and dug some more. Good grief. Besides the six-packs of soda, Melanie had a box of granola bars and some peanut butter crackers. What a stash. Christina grabbed a soda for Eliza, and on second thought, took one for herself, too. She closed Melanie's trunk and walked back to Flash's stall.

"Here you go. Hope you like root beer."

Eliza stepped out from behind Flash and took the can. "Thanks." Even in the dim light, her eyes were puffy and red. Christina couldn't help but feel a little sorry for her.

"I bet he'll be fine," Christina said. "We've had a lot of horses colic, and only a couple of them died."

"That's supposed to make me feel better?"

"But that's out of *all* the horses that have come through our barn," Christina explained. "And people are always shipping us mares for breeding. A lot of horses colic when they travel to a new place." She paused. "I wonder if that's why Flash got sick? Maybe he didn't drink enough water or something because it was different from home."

Eliza wiped her nose on the sleeve of her T-shirt. "Well, it wasn't the hay or grain. I always smell them to make sure they aren't moldy." She sniffed again. "You don't have any tissues, do you?"

"How about a paper towel? I've got a roll in my trunk." Christina tore off a sheet and passed it to Eliza.

"Thanks."

Christina left Eliza to mop her face and blow her nose in private. She grabbed her tack bucket, ran some water into it, and started working on Trib's bit.

Eliza came out of the stall. She shoved the paper towel in her pocket and leaned against the door. "I guess I should thank you for what you did."

Christina waited, not sure what was going to come next.

"You probably saved his life. If he had died, I don't know what I would have done."

"Don't think about it," Christina said, watching Eliza's eyes fill with tears.

"I have to," she answered through clenched teeth. "He doesn't even belong to me."

Christina stopped rubbing the bit. "What?"

Eliza blinked and looked away. "Flash isn't my horse."

8

"WHAT DO YOU MEAN HE'S NOT YOUR HORSE?"

Eliza kicked at the dirt with her shoe while Christina waited. When she finally raised her chin, her voice came out all trembly.

"A woman at my barn is trying to sell him because he's too hard for her to handle. My instructor talked her into letting me bring him to camp so he could have more experience. And because she knew I needed a horse to ride."

"But you've been coming to Saddlebrook for years. Don't you have a horse?" Eliza didn't ride like someone who only rode once a week at a lesson.

"I do, but he's too old for this much work now. My instructor uses him to give lessons to beginners."

"Why don't *you* buy Flash then? You guys are perfect for each other."

Eliza looked down at her feet again. "I've been baby-sitting and saving up all winter, but I don't have nearly enough money."

"Won't your parents help?"

"They were going to, but then someone bought the company my dad worked for and he lost his job."

"He got fired?"

"No," Eliza said, her voice suddenly angry. "He got laid off. There's a difference." She shook her head, brushing the loose hairs back from her face as she turned away. "Oh, never mind. Forget I said anything."

Christina stood up. "But there must be *something* you can do."

"What?" Eliza snapped, spinning back around. "*I* don't have lots of money. *I* can't have everything I want."

Christina stepped back. She could feel her cheeks getting red. "Are you saying I do?"

"Yeah." Eliza just stared as if she were waiting for Christina to deny it.

Christina crossed her arms. "Well, if I could have anything, I sure wouldn't be stuck in a stall next to you."

Eliza rolled her eyes. "You rich kids don't know anything," she said in a disgusted voice.

"I'm not rich."

"Then what do *you* call it? You have your own Thoroughbred and practically a whole tack shop in that custom-made trunk of yours. To say nothing of a groom that delivers it for you."

Is *that* what was bothering her? Christina was steamed. "It's not my fault my parents are in the horse business. I'd much rather have had *them* drive me to camp instead of someone who works for them, but they were too busy. And sure, I've got a lot of tack and stuff, but most of it is stuff my parents don't use anymore."

"Oh, forget it," Eliza said, turning to go back into Flash's stall.

"No." Christina threw the sponge into the bucket. "You've been snotty to me ever since I came, and I haven't done anything to you. And for your information, the reason my tack trunk is so big is because my father built it for me and it turned out bigger than he planned. But I guess that makes it custom-made." Christina took a few steps away, then turned back.

"And I know I'm lucky to have Sterling, but don't make me out to be a stuck-up rich kid. I work hard around our farm and so do my parents. I'm sorry that you don't have a horse right now and I'm sorry your father lost his job. But if anyone is acting stuck-up around here, it's you."

She emptied the dirty water and stuffed Trib's bridle back in Melanie's trunk. She was sick and tired of Eliza.

"Wait," Eliza said as Christina started to leave.

She hesitated, then turned.

"I'm sorry."

Christina was still trembling with anger. Her face

felt frozen as she stared at the knot in the wood behind Eliza's shoulder.

"I know I've been awful. I know. But when you showed up with everything I've always wished I had . . ." Her voice trailed off and she picked at the dirt under her fingernails.

Christina waited.

Eliza took a deep breath and looked up again. "I was jealous. All I've ever wanted is to work with horses," she said with a wobbly voice. "It's the only thing I really care about. I know it sounds awful, but I'd give anything to have parents like yours who could understand how I feel." Eliza sagged onto her trunk and leaned back against the barn wall.

"The only reason I had Cinders—my old horse— was that a neighbor gave him to me when she went to college. My family helps out with the shoeing and vet bills and all, but they could care less about my riding. They think it's something I'll outgrow." Eliza managed a small smile and Christina found herself smiling back.

"I come home from working all Saturday at the barn—that's how I pay for my lessons—and the family room will be dark because they've pulled the curtains closed and are watching football or soccer. I know my father wishes I were interested in basketball or something useful that could get me into college on a sports scholarship. They just don't understand."

Christina hoisted herself onto the railing. "I know what you mean," she said. "My parents expected me to love racing just because they do. It took a lot of begging before they'd let me sell my racehorse so I could buy Sterling. And I don't think they really believe that I'm going to be able to get very far training her."

"Really?" Eliza said. "I could help you if you want."

Christina was about to say no, not believing Eliza would do anything nice for her. But something in Eliza's face told her she meant it. "You will?"

"Sure. Sterling's a nice horse."

"You think so?"

"Yeah."

"Sometimes I worry she won't make a good event horse, though." Christina jumped down and crossed the aisle to rub Sterling's nose. "She started out okay, but now it seems like we're always fighting each other."

"Flash was like that, too, at first. He gets away with murder with his owner. It took a while before we really learned to communicate." Eliza looked at her watch and jumped up. "It's time to walk him again."

Christina stepped forward. "You want some help?"

"Sure," Eliza said.

The next few hours went by quickly. Christina lost count of the number of times they led Flash around the green. As they talked together, it was hard to believe that Eliza was the same person who had gone out of her way to be so mean to Christina just the day before.

Christina told Eliza about falling off Sterling and breaking her wrist when she was trying to school over a jump. Eliza described the first time she saw Flash, and how terrible he acted whenever his owner, Lois Murphy, rode him.

"Did he ever rear or buck with you?" Christina asked after hearing about the times he dumped Lois.

"A little," Eliza admitted, rummaging in her trunk until she found the bag of embroidery thread for making bracelets. "He just doesn't like to be bottled up, and Lois is always hanging onto his mouth, trying to force him into a dressage frame. When he goes faster to get away, she gets scared and clamps down even harder. She needs a less sensitive horse."

"But how did you learn to make him behave?"

Eliza thought for a minute. "I think it's that I *ask* him rather than force him. When horses don't do what you want, chances are it's because they don't really understand what you're asking. My instructor works a lot with me on communicating with my seat as well as my legs and hands. She thinks that with a horse like Flash, I might be able to make the Young Riders team in a year or two." Eliza looked down at the bracelet she was starting.

Christina didn't want her to get all sad again. "Hey, can you teach me how to braid like that?"

"I guess so. But we'll need another safety pin."

Christina had one in her tack box.

"Is there anything you *don't* have in there?" Eliza asked. But she was smiling.

Christina had to start a couple of times before she got the hang of it. She had never had to juggle so many threads at once, but that was what made the bracelets different. When she was halfway finished, she had an idea.

"You know, one of the craft people at the fair tonight was talking about selling stuff at the farmers' market in town. I bet you could sell a bunch of these bracelets there."

"You think so?" Eliza said, raising her eyebrows.

"Sure. You saw how many kids here wanted to buy them. It would give you more money for your Flash fund."

Eliza's face dropped. "Lois is already advertising him and I haven't earned even half her asking price. There's no way I can make enough money in time."

"But she might not find a buyer for him right away. You said yourself he's sensitive and doesn't click with everyone. You've got to keep trying." Christina got an inspiration. "I could help make bracelets. And I bet Melanie and Jennifer would make them, too. Then you'd have lots to sell."

"I guess my mother could drop off more embroidery thread."

"Maybe if your parents see how much money you're earning, they'll help you out. Sometimes my mother will match my money when I'm saving up for something expensive."

Eliza shook her head. "I know my parents can't do that. They didn't even have enough money to send me to camp this year. If Ms. Perkins hadn't offered me a scholarship, I wouldn't have been able to come."

"I still think there must be some way you could come up with the money," Christina said. "Maybe if all of us—"

Eliza stopped her. "*Please* don't tell anybody else. Ms. Perkins is the only person who knows about the scholarship and everything, and I want to keep it that way." Her lower lip started to tremble. "I just want to pretend Flash is my horse for the rest of camp, and I can't do that if everyone is feeling sorry for me."

"I'm sorry," Christina said, then slapped her hand over her mouth. "Sorry, I said sorry."

That made them both laugh. Flash even came to the door to see what was going on.

When Ms. Perkins came out to relieve them at three o'clock and said Flash looked a lot better, Eliza and Christina sent her back to bed, insisting that they could manage.

"Our parents won't mind," Christina said as Ms. Perkins began to protest. "We stay up all night at slumber parties, anyway."

At four-thirty when the birds were waking up and the sky seemed a tiny bit less black, Flash finally relieved himself.

"I've never seen anyone so excited about cleaning out a stall," Christina teased as Eliza danced around with the pitchfork. But she was relieved, too. Flash was out of danger now.

They slept through the morning lesson and lunch. By the time they woke up, it was midafternoon and all the kids had gone to the lake.

"Only I had to stay behind," Dana informed them, "because Ms. Perkins didn't want to leave you alone."

It was hard to feel sorry for Dana when she was such a grump.

"Can we go down to the barn?" Eliza asked. "The vet said I should take Flash out for a walk later."

Dana finally agreed to let them, but only after Eliza bribed her with a candy bar. When they led their horses out of the stalls, Dana was stretched out on the porch swing with a soda and a magazine.

"Grab your bridle and helmet," Eliza whispered. "But don't let Dana see them."

Christina followed Eliza's suit and stuffed her helmet under her shirt.

"Come on," Eliza directed. She and Flash headed behind the hay barn toward the river with Christina and Sterling following. Christina couldn't even tell Flash had ever been sick.

"No fair if everyone but us gets to go swimming," Eliza said as soon as they were out of sight of the house. "Put on your bridle and let's go."

Eliza gave Christina a leg up onto Sterling's back

101

before swinging up on Flash. "Have you ever ridden her bareback?"

"No. But I used to ride Trib bareback all the time."

"Good," Eliza said.

As they came in sight of the stream, Christina asked, "So what do we do? Take turns holding the horses while one of us swims?"

Eliza wiggled her eyebrows. "We're all going in."

"Don't hold your breath," Christina said. "I told you how much trouble I've had with Sterling and water."

"I want to try something. You gave me the idea with Flash last night." Eliza unwound the lead line she had tied around her waist. "I'm going to try to pony him in."

"But I've tried following other horses. It doesn't work."

"This is different." Eliza brought Flash next to Christina, then leaned down to clip the hook around Sterling's bit. "Now drop your reins and just be a passenger."

They practiced ponying Sterling around a little before heading toward the stream. Christina felt as if she were a little kid riding a pony at a carnival.

"Now don't do anything but sit when we go toward the water," Eliza said over her shoulder. "I want Sterling to pay attention to Flash, not you."

Christina hooked her hands behind her head. "I'm just here for the ride," she said.

Eliza stopped Flash just at the edge of the water and let him drink. Sterling stepped closer to watch. Flash wandered further in and Sterling followed.

"I can't believe she did that," Christina said.

"Sometimes you just have to vary the routine," Eliza answered. "Let's go downstream a ways."

Eliza still led. "That way, it's like Flash is in charge and Sterling doesn't have to worry. I read a book once about a guy who spent years studying wild mustangs, and he learned that even horses who have never been wild still behave like they're part of a herd."

"I've heard of him," Christina said. "Isn't he the one from California who is so good at talking to horses—he can ride a wild mustang after handling it an hour? And he does it without hurting them at all?"

"That's him." Eliza got a dreamy look in her eyes. "I'd sure like to work for him sometime—learn how he does that."

"Me too," Christina said, nodding.

They played in the water for half an hour, and by the time they stopped, Christina could ride Sterling up and down the bank without Flash.

"Boy, I hope she remembers how to do this again," Christina said. "Everyone was starting to doubt that Sterling would be my event horse." It seemed disloyal to add that she had been wondering the same thing.

"It's too soon to tell yet," Eliza said. "But I don't see why she wouldn't. She's a beautiful mover and built right to jump. If you don't rush her, I bet it won't be long before you two connect."

"Like you and Flash?"

Eliza stroked Flash's ebony neck. "Yeah," she said in a soft voice. "If you really love her."

When they put the horses away, Dana hollered from the house. "Hey, Eliza. Phone."

"I'm going to the kennel," Christina said. "If you want, we can make more bracelets."

"Okay," Eliza said, smiling as she headed up the porch steps. "I'll be there in a minute."

It was closer to ten minutes before Eliza opened the screened door. Christina could tell she'd been crying.

"What's wrong?"

Eliza covered her eyes with her hand and her shoulders started to shake. "That was Lois," she said, sobbing. "She thinks she's found a buyer for Flash. The man's coming the day after tomorrow to try him out."

9

"IT'S NOT FAIR," CHRISTINA SAID, HANDING ELIZA THE BOX of tissues. They were sitting cross-legged on the top bunk.

Eliza blew her nose. "Flash is her horse."

"I think she should sell him to you cheap. After all, if it wasn't for you, he'd still be rotten."

"Don't remind me," Eliza said. She flipped her braid over one shoulder and rubbed the end between her fingers. "Lois says she has to get enough from him so she can buy a new horse."

"I don't think someone like her should have a horse," Christina fumed. "Not when she treats him like . . . like a car or something. Doesn't she have any feelings?"

Eliza didn't say anything.

"Well, we can't just sit here," Christina said. "We need to do something."

"There isn't anything to do," Eliza said. "I've run out of time."

Christina blew the hair out of her eyes. "You can't give up. You don't even know if this guy's going to like him. Maybe Flash will be so bad, he'll scare the guy away."

"Yeah, maybe." Eliza didn't sound hopeful.

"Come on," Christina said. "Let's make bracelets. If we hurry, I bet we can get four more done by dinner."

Eliza uncrossed her legs. "I can't right now." She swallowed hard. "If you don't mind, I need to spend some time alone with Flash."

She jumped off the bed and turned as she got to the screen door. "Thanks."

Christina had never seen a sadder face. Just yesterday, she knew she would have taken the opportunity to spread Eliza's bad news all around the camp just to get back at her. But now the girls were actually friends and Christina really wanted to help. It was amazing how quickly things could change.

After dinner, some of the kids watched a video of the 1996 Badminton Horse Trials, one of the biggest international three-day events in the world.

"Aren't you going to watch?" Christina asked as Eliza hung back.

"I don't feel like it tonight," she said.

Christina followed her to the door. "It might take your mind off . . . things." She glanced over her shoulder to make sure no one was listening.

"I'm really tired. I think I'll just go to bed."

Eliza was asleep, or at least pretending to be, when Christina, Melanie, and Jennifer trooped in at nine o'clock. For once, Melanie and Jennifer didn't talk a lot after lights out, and before long, Christina could hear their steady breathing.

She sat up in her bunk. "Eliza," she whispered. "You awake?"

When there wasn't an answer, Christina turned her pillow over and tried to get comfortable. She didn't know how Eliza could have fallen asleep already. Christina had slept so late today, she wasn't even tired.

Poor Eliza. Christina couldn't even imagine what she'd do if someone threatened to take Sterling away. If only there were a way to buy Flash for Eliza. But where could she find that kind of money?

Christina tried to remember all the times she'd earned money. When she was little, she'd put on puppet shows for her parents and charged them fifty cents each for a seat. Christina bought quite a lot of ice cream before her parents suggested she find another way to earn money.

Maybe she could get the other campers together and put on some kind of a show. But what could they do that people would pay money to see? Besides, Eliza didn't want anyone to know about her and Flash, though Christina guessed they'd figure it out soon enough when that buyer came.

Maybe they could have a talent show. The one at

school last year filled the auditorium for two nights. Of course, the audience mostly consisted of parents, brothers, sisters, and lots of students. It wouldn't work at camp—not with only twenty campers. They'd need to get someone famous to perform to sell enough tickets, and she didn't know anyone in show business.

Wait a minute. Uncle Will, Melanie's father, was in the music business. He worked with famous rock groups all the time. Maybe he could help.

By the time Christina dragged Melanie out of bed the next morning, she had it all planned.

"I need to talk to you," she whispered.

Melanie yawned. "So talk."

"Not here," Christina said. "I mean where no one can overhear us."

"You planning to kidnap Dana and hold her for ransom, or something?" Melanie said, looking at Christina out of the corner of her eye.

"Just hurry up and get dressed. We'll talk on the way to the barn."

Melanie's curiosity must have been sufficiently aroused, because she met Christina in record time. "So what's with all the cloak-and-dagger stuff?" she asked as Christina pulled her toward the stadium field.

"First you have to promise not to tell Eliza any-thing."

Melanie rolled her eyes. "I don't *know* anything."

"Just promise, okay?"

"Okay. Cross my heart and hope to fall off Trib right in front of Sean," she said, giggling.

"This is serious." Christina stopped and turned to Melanie. "If we don't do something, Eliza is going to lose Flash."

For once, Melanie shut up enough for Christina to fill her in on what was happening.

"And I came up with a perfect way to make enough money so Eliza can buy Flash. Only we're going to need your father."

"Dad? I can't even get him to buy *me* a horse."

"That's because he thinks you're too crazy," Christina said.

"True," Melanie admitted, not at all offended.

"This is different, anyway. If we can get your dad to have one of his rock groups hold a benefit concert, we could easily raise enough money to give to Eliza."

Melanie's eyes lit up. "A rock concert? Here? Cool."

"The band could set up on the Irish Bank over there," Christina said, pointing across the stadium field to where a squared mound stood three feet off the ground. "People could bring blankets to sit on. It would be great."

"I bet I could get him to do it," Melanie said. "He's organized concerts for charity before."

"We shouldn't call it charity, though," Christina said quickly, "or Eliza would never take it." She hooked her thumbs in the belt loops of her breeches. "I know. We could say it's for the Young Riders program. They're always looking for sponsors to raise money for clinics and traveling to the nationals and everything. I bet Eliza and Flash will make our Area VIII team in a couple of years, anyway."

Melanie nodded her head. "Sounds good to me."

They decided to check with Uncle Will first. Melanie used the phone in Perky's office to call her father while Christina stood guard by the door.

"Hi, Dad," Melanie said. "No, nothing's wrong. Why do you always ask that?" She made a face at Christina.

"Camp is great. I'm learning a bunch. We went out on the stadium course yesterday and you should have seen the fences we jumped."

Christina wished she hadn't slept through that lesson. "Hurry up," she whispered, checking the hall.

"Listen, Dad. I have something important to ask you."

Christina held her breath as Melanie made her pitch. She had to admit, her cousin was convincing.

"You will!" Melanie's eyes were wide as she nodded at Christina. "Okay, I'll put her on." She covered the mouthpiece. "Get Perky. Quick."

Christina caught Ms. Perkins just as she was heading out the door. On the way back, Christina quickly explained their idea to raise money for the Young Riders.

"Ms. Perkins, here," she said, picking up the phone. "Oh yes, Mr. Graham. Melanie's fitting in quite nicely."

Melanie put her hand to her face and shook her head, groaning.

"Yes. Yes," Ms. Perkins said, listening. "Yes, that's quite right. It costs a pretty penny to get our young people properly trained. But the United States has no hope of improving our international standing if we don't. We've had two campers who went on to compete in the Olympics, you know."

Christina's nails were digging into her palms, she was so excited.

"Well, that's very generous of you. Of course, I'd have to check with our board of directors first, but I would imagine they would be agreeable to a fundraiser. . . . Sunday evening will be quite good. I should think most everyone will stay on after the Quadrille Ride and Parents' Picnic in the afternoon. Now with your ads on the radio, how many more people would you hope to attract?" Ms. Perkins put her hand to her throat as she listened. "Oh, really?" she said. "I'll pop down to our local police department then. We'll need help with all those cars."

Melanie took the phone when Ms. Perkins was finished. "Thanks a million, Dad. You're the best." She smiled and nodded. "Love you, too. Can't wait to see you on Sunday."

"Well done," Ms. Perkins said when Melanie hung up. "You certainly know how to stir things up."

"Thank you," Melanie said gravely. "I've had plenty of practice."

Of course, it was almost impossible not to tell everyone about the concert, but Ms. Perkins explained she'd need to get permission from the people who were in charge of Saddlebrook before the concert was definite.

After lunch, everyone met on the porch.

"Our lecture this afternoon will take place in the large dressage arena where Nathan, Jody, Adrianne, and Dana will demonstrate a quadrille."

"Is that geometry?" Melanie said, narrowing her eyes. Everyone laughed.

"Only in that *quadra* is Latin for square," Ms. Perkins said with a straight face.

Melanie gasped. "Latin! Now I'm really sunk."

"As I was saying . . ." Ms. Perkins waited until everyone was quiet again. "It is a tradition for students to team up in groups of four and prepare a quadrille ride to perform in front of the parents on Parents' Day each year. Would anyone like to explain what is involved with riding a quadrille?"

Rachel raised her hand. "It's almost like a dance where four riders are in the dressage ring at once. The hard part is keeping the horses synchronized so they look like mirror images of themselves as they go down separate sides from each other."

Dylan jumped in. "If you've watched any old westerns with the United States Cavalry, just picture the way they rode in formations."

"It's really cool when two of the horses trot down

one diagonal and two trot down the other," Jennifer added. "You have to time it just right so that the horses take turns crossing X at the center."

"And if they don't, ca-rash!" Sean said, rubbing his hands and looking like a mad scientist. Jennifer pushed him with her shoulder, giggling.

"You'll understand better when you see our demonstration," Ms. Perkins said.

"Who will we ride with?" Christina asked.

"You'll be riding with your teams," Ms. Perkins said. "The winning quadrille will earn twenty-five extra points and second place will earn fifteen points."

The mention of points started everyone buzzing. Eliza whispered to Christina. "It would really help our score if we won. As of this morning, we're second to last."

Christina nodded, glad to see her showing some interest. Eliza had hardly spoken all morning.

Jody and the other instructors came out of the barns on their horses. Ms. Perkins clapped her hands to get everyone's attention. "Let's move to the arena."

Jody led the way on her Hanoverian, Queen of Hearts. The chestnut mare known around the barn as Queenie certainly moved like royalty. With head up and eyes alert, her long legs strode down the driveway with quiet dignity.

Nathan and Adrianne followed, riding side by side. Though his horse was the tallest of the group,

Nathan's long legs hung a little below the horse's girth.

"Gulliver is over seventeen hands high," Jennifer said, "and Nathan makes him look small."

Christina appraised the big-boned Thoroughbred with tawny circles of gold dappling his glossy dark brown hair. She could see how easily Nathan's seat followed when Gulliver danced to one side. Without even interrupting his conversation with Adrianne, Nathan steadied the horse, quietly bringing him back to a long, swingy walk.

Adrianne's gelding, Peppermint Twist, was as round and light as Gulliver was rangy and dark. Christina knew that Pepper's father was a Thoroughbred colt that her father had sold years before. Adrianne's family owned the Connamara mare that was the gelding's mother, and Adrianne had trained Pepper from the time he was a foal. His nickname, Pepper, suited him because his white hair was peppered with black flecks.

Dana and her Morgan horse, Fantasia, brought up the rear. Fantasia was pretty in a prancey way. She stepped quickly, bringing her hooves up high as if she were walking through deep mud. Christina personally thought that horses like her looked better marching in a parade than performing dressage.

The four riders warmed up—walking, trotting, and cantering in small circles outside the dressage arena—while Ms. Perkins talked more about the quadrilles.

"You may use one of the USDF tests—those are ones issued by the United States Dressage Federation—or your team may make up their own. If you do make up your own, you will have to write it down so Mrs. Bruder will be able to score you."

"Can we still ride to music if we want?" Sean asked.

Christina's ears pricked up. Sterling liked riding to music. She remembered the few moments at their last dressage show when someone turned a boom box on and Sterling started to move to the rhythm of the song.

"You may use music." Ms. Perkins paused. "But given the short time we have to prepare these rides, you might want to just concentrate on the riding. It takes a lot of time to plan a musical ride, or freestyle as it's more correctly called. Every time your horse goes from a walk to a trot, or a trot to a canter, the tempo of his movement changes. A walk is four beats, a trot is two beats, and a canter is three beats. It's time-consuming to find music selections that fit with each tempo and to put them together to fit your quadrille."

"Would we have to come up with the music ourselves?" Sean asked.

"You'll need a recording to put on the PA system."

"No, I mean do *we* have to make the tapes?"

Christina had never seen Sean look so intense.

Ms. Perkins thought about it. "You may use tapes that have been commercially made for this purpose, if that's what you mean. But bear in mind that they might not suit your horse's way of moving." She raised her voice and called to the riders, "Are you ready?"

As Jody and the rest got themselves grouped to enter the arena, Christina saw Sean waving his hands as he talked to Dylan.

"Rachel, Bekka, over here," he called, flagging the rest of his team. When he noticed Christina watching, he pulled them around to the other side of the ring. It was obvious he didn't want to be overheard. What were they planning?

Her attention was pulled back when Nathan said, "Okay . . . *now.*" She watched, impressed, as the four riders entered the arena in pairs: Nathan and Jody in front with Adrianne and Dana following. It was wonderful to watch as they split away from each other at X, only to reunite at the C end of the arena as they turned down the center line in pairs once again.

Not that everything went so smoothly. Queenie put her ears back and made a face at Gulliver, causing him to shy away for a second before Nathan's long legs took command again. And Dana let Fantasia break into a canter twice when she was supposed to be doing a lengthening at a trot. *She wasn't nearly as hotshot a rider as she pretended to be,* Christina thought.

By the time they halted—four abreast—and saluted,

Christina was shivery with excitement. Riding a quadrille was going to be a blast.

"Did you see how Dana messed up?" Melanie gloated on the way back to the barn.

"Just wait. It's harder than it looks," Eliza said. Her voice was all gloomy again.

"I wish I knew what Sean was up to." Jennifer was in front of the three of them, walking backward. "Look at him."

Christina turned around. Sure enough, Sean, Dylan, Rachel, and Bekka were huddled together with Sean looking over his shoulder. Christina didn't like the way Rachel was looking up at Dylan as she hung onto his every word.

"Remember last year when his mother was mad because his team only came in third?" Eliza said to Jennifer.

"That's nothing," she said. "Sean told me he got grounded for a month after he got five A's and one B on his report card last winter. And the B was in chemistry." Jennifer rolled her eyes. "I'm glad my parents aren't like that."

"You'd better stop talking and get tacked up," Dana said as she rode up beside them. "The afternoon lessons start in twenty minutes."

"Fantasia looked good," Melanie said. "Too bad she kept cantering to keep up."

Her face was innocent and sincere, but Christina knew her cousin well enough to know when she was

117

deliberately poking a stick down a bee's hole. Dana didn't look sure whether she was getting a compliment or not. When Christina grinned, Dana frowned.

"Don't think you're going to be able to do as well. I've seen how your horse goes. She'll probably freak out and wreck it for your whole team."

Eliza moved in. "Give it a rest, Dana. You're supposed to be with us, not against us."

It was nice of Eliza to stick up for her, but Christina was still mad. It didn't matter what Dana said, or what Sean and Dylan were planning. Her team was going to win if it was the last thing she did.

10

Instead of riding with regular groups for the afternoon lesson, everyone was going to practice quadrilles with their teams. Nathan stopped by Christina's end of the barn while they were getting ready.

"I reserved the stadium field for us," he said. "When you all finish saddling up, meet me there."

"Nathan is *sooo* cute," Jennifer said as soon as he was out of sight. "He reminds me of Superman."

"You mean Clark Kent, right? They both wear glasses," Melanie said. Then she burst out laughing. "Look who Team Five got stuck with."

Christina almost choked when she saw Dana standing with her hands on her hips across the green. Dylan and Sean didn't look very happy.

After they were tacked up, Christina and the others rode to the end of the stadium field where someone had set up a short dressage ring using white buckets with letters painted on them as markers.

"Okay, Team Three," Nathan said after he made sure he knew everyone's name. "We'll start by riding in a ride."

"Say what?" Melanie asked.

"A ride." Nathan smiled and Christina could see what Jennifer meant by Superman. His whole face lit up and adorable dimples appeared on each of his cheeks.

"That's what they call it in England when you ride in a line, keeping one horse's length between you." Nathan pushed his glasses further back on his nose with his index finger. "This will give you practice in regulating your horse's stride so he doesn't run up on, or fall back from, the horse in front of him. Why don't you lead the way, Eliza? Then Christina, Jennifer, and Melanie can follow in that order."

Christina turned into place behind Eliza. As they walked along, she felt as if she were playing follow the leader.

"Prepare to trot," Nathan said from the middle of the arena. "Now trot, rising."

Sterling was quiet when Christina closed her legs and asked for a trot. Flash's stride was close enough to Sterling's so that Christina had no trouble keeping the right distance away. She glanced over her shoulder at the other two. Jennifer and Geronimo were steady behind her, and Melanie waved from the back. This wasn't so hard.

"K-X-M, change the rein," Nathan shouted.

Christina looked for the K marker in the corner where they'd turn to go up the diagonal and change direction. When Sterling took the turn, she got too close to Flash. Sterling stuck her nose up in the air as Christina tried to hold her back.

"Next time, ride her further into the corner before you turn," Nathan told Christina. "The reason she got too close to Flash is that she cut the corner."

They worked for a half hour in the ride. It seemed as though Nathan watched every move they made.

"You need to sit before you close your fingers on the reins when you ask for a walk, Melanie," Nathan said. "Turn your body to the inside, not the outside, as you ride that canter circle, Christina." And, "Bring your chin back, Jennifer. You look like you're trying to put yourself on the bit when you're curled over like that."

"Did I say Superman?" Jennifer whispered when they stopped for a breather. "I should have said Attila the Hun."

"Not a bad start," Nathan said, taking off his glasses and wiping his brow. His face looked bare without them. "Let's go over by the trees and I'll read you the first Introductory Quadrille Test while you cool off. Then we'll ride through it a couple of times and call it a day."

The test sounded easy under the trees, but riding it was another matter.

"I thought you told me to track left," Melanie said.

"Track right," Nathan said. "Otherwise you're going to run into Eliza."

They laughed so much, Christina's stomach hurt. "Maybe we should just dress up and call ourselves the Four Stooges," she said after they got tangled for the umpteenth time.

"You'll get it," Nathan said. "You're just paying too much attention to your own horses and not enough attention to what's going on around you." He pointed to Melanie. "And we're going to have to put a helmet on Trib if you don't stop looking down instead of where you're going."

"I was concentrating," Melanie protested.

"On what? Your nail polish?" Jennifer teased.

Christina was tired but happy as she followed the others back to the barn. It was fun to be part of a team.

Everyone was so busy trying to top each other's funny quadrille stories that when Ms. Perkins came in to make an announcement during dinner, Christina almost forgot what it was about.

"We have a special event scheduled Sunday evening after our Parents' Picnic. You may want to let your parents know about it so they can plan accordingly." When Ms. Perkins told them about the benefit rock concert, a collective cheer filled the room.

"Who's playing?" Jennifer asked.

Melanie spoke up. "We don't know yet. Dad's got to check out some schedules before he decides, but whoever he sends will be good. He's got a lot of big-name groups."

After dinner, Christina had to drag Melanie away from the house. She could tell her cousin was enjoying being the center of attention.

"Come on," Christina said. "Eliza is going to get a copy of the quadrille tests from Ms. Perkins so we can decide which one we want to do."

"Can't we take a break from horses for one night?" Melanie said. "This is getting a little old."

"Look," Christina hissed. "Rachel, Bekka, Sean, and Dylan have already left. I heard them talking about meeting at the carriage house."

Melanie's eyebrows shot up. "Sounds like a party to me. How come they can have girls in their room but we can't have boys?"

Christina shoved her. "Get your mind out of the gutter," she said, even though she'd had the same suspicions. Christina could hardly say two sentences to Dylan without Rachel right there, barging in. Eliza said she chased him around a lot last year, too. It was sickening how much attention Dylan and Sean got just because they were boys.

"It's something to do with the quadrille," Christina continued. "Sean was asking Ms. Perkins a bunch of stuff while you were going on about your father's rock groups."

"They're not all rock, you know."

"Whatever," Christina said, hoping Uncle Will

would send a group that people would want to hear. "Just find Jennifer and meet us by the stadium field."

The mosquitoes were starting to come out by the time everyone showed up. "Okay," Eliza said, taking charge. "I think that Novice Test 1 would be the best one for this group."

"I think we should do a harder test," Jennifer said. "Geronimo does a great lengthening."

Eliza turned to Melanie. "Does Trib have a lengthening?"

"Only when he's running away with me in a trot," Melanie said, laughing.

Christina shook her head. "He doesn't, really. And Sterling speeds up a lot of the time when I ask her to lengthen, or falls into a canter. I don't think we're ready yet."

Eliza looked at Jennifer. "We'd be better off with Novice, then."

Jennifer looked disappointed, but she said, "Fine with me."

"The first step is to try the test by ourselves, on foot," Eliza said. "If we can synchronize ourselves on the ground, then we'll have a better chance of doing it when we're riding. Let's just walk it the first time. I'll read the directions as we go."

Even the small 40-meter-by-20-meter dressage arena felt big when they were on foot. By the time they started jogging (for trotting) and galloping (for canter), Christina really appreciated how fit the horses were.

Melanie tossed her head and whinnied. "I used to do this in elementary school," she said as she galloped. "We'd pretend we were wild horses at recess."

"Let's try it one more time," Eliza said. She was a bigger slave driver than Nathan.

"No more." Jennifer fell to the ground in a faint. Melanie dove beside her and landed in a heap.

"We'd better quit or we won't be able to move tomorrow." Christina's voice was apologetic.

Eliza slumped. "I guess you're right," she said, suddenly losing all her enthusiasm.

Christina could have kicked herself for mentioning the next day and making Eliza remember someone was coming to see Flash.

At breakfast the next morning, Ms. Perkins announced that they'd be riding with their regular lesson groups first, and in the afternoon they would practice the quadrilles in their teams. And when Jody told her riding group that they were having a jumping lesson on the cross-country course, Christina forgot all about Eliza's problem.

"Did I put these things on right?" Melanie asked as she led Trib out of his stall.

Christina checked the padded splint boots to make sure they were fastened the right way on Trib's legs. The boots were to keep him from cutting himself with his shoe if he slipped over the rough ground.

They had to be put on just right so that they wouldn't slide around or restrict his blood.

"They're fine," Christina said, putting on her red safety vest and patting the Velcro into place. Sterling's splint boots were red, too. Christina liked the way they looked against Sterling's gray dapples.

"I feel like a football player in this," Melanie complained as she looked at the padded foam vest that, except for being royal blue, was just like Christina's.

"It's not that bulky," Christina said. "Anyway, you'll be glad you have it if you fall off Trib and he steps on you."

Melanie shook her head. "I don't know about this cross-country stuff, Cuz. Show jumping is sounding safer all the time."

Christina laughed as she snapped on her helmet and pulled the stirrups down on Sterling's saddle. "Okay, girl," she said, running her hand along the mare's broad chest. "This is what we've been waiting for."

They started out by hard galloping around a small field as soon as they'd loosened up the horses. Sterling got excited following the others. She sped up as if she were in a race.

"Shorten your reins a little, Christina," Jody called. "And plant them further up her neck. You have to slow her down with your *seat*. If you pull, she'll just lean on you and run more."

Christina tried what she said, and when she sat

back, Sterling slowed down. This was the greatest. It almost felt as though she and Sterling were one.

Jody had them trot, then canter over a long, fallen tree. At first Sterling tried to fly over it, but after three or four times she settled down and jumped as if it were no big deal.

"Nice job, Christina. I like the way you're keeping your upper body back and letting Sterling close the angle when she jumps. Rachel, watch the way Christina is jumping. This is what I'm trying to get you to do."

So, there, Christina thought with satisfaction. Rachel might be the prettiest girl at the camp, but she wasn't the best rider by a long shot.

After they finished jumping the tree, Jody took them down a wide logging trail that opened into a larger field. She pointed to the stone wall next to the road.

"Who wants to go first over this one?"

Christina was feeling pretty confident. "I will."

"Okay then. When you come down the road, Sterling won't see the wall at first. You'll need to swing out to the left so you'll have plenty of room to turn right toward the wall. We'll help you out by taking the rest of the horses on the other side."

Christina's heart was beating hard as she walked Sterling back in the direction they had come. Sterling jigged a little, nervous about leaving the other horses. "Okay, girl," Christina said, stopping before turning her around. "Do me proud."

Sterling wheeled as if she'd been shot out of a cannon. Christina could do little more than steer as they galloped down the road. *Sit back, sit back,* she told herself, but it was easier said than done.

When they got to the place where they needed to swing left, Christina rode a firm half halt. "Whoa," she commanded, sitting back and squeezing as hard as she could.

To her amazement, Sterling rocked back and turned neatly on her haunches. Her head came up and her ears were forward as she faced the stone wall. She took two strides then left the ground in a jump that nearly took Christina's breath away. It felt like minutes before they touched the grass on the other side with Sterling galloping on, eagerly pointed toward a white coop.

"Whoa," Christina called again as they flashed by the other horses. This time Sterling ignored her half halt. Christina had to pull her head around and canter in a large circle before Sterling finally listened enough to slow down.

"Well," Jody said as Christina sheepishly walked back. "We've got to get you some brakes."

"I don't know what's wrong with her," Christina said. "She was never this wild on cross-country before."

Jody smiled. "She's developing some confidence in her jumping, I'd say. Even though she went into that wall way too fast for elementary, or even novice division, her form was quite nice. If she stays sound, this may be a horse you could take intermediate some day."

Jody's words echoed in her ears. Intermediate fences were the ones that made her spine tingle when she looked at pictures in magazines or watched videos of the big events. And she was sure Sterling would stay sound enough to get that far in her training. Hadn't her mother said Sterling's conformation was very nearly perfect?

By the time the cross-country lesson was over and they were walking through the stadium field, Christina was floating on a cloud. "You are the best," she said, leaning to give Sterling a hug around the neck. Sterling's back rose as she whinnied across the driveway. Christina looked up and saw Flash's glossy black hindquarters in the distance.

"Let's go tell Eliza what a champion jumper you are," Christina said, squeezing Sterling into a trot. "Eliza, wait up."

But when they got closer, Christina realized that it wasn't Eliza leading Flash. *It must be Flash's owner, Lois.*

And that meant the man walking next to her was probably the buyer.

11

"Uh-oh," Melanie said as she rode Trib up and stopped beside Sterling. "Is that who I think it is?"

"Probably," Christina said. She had told Melanie about Flash's owner bringing a possible buyer out to ride Flash, but she hadn't told anyone else.

"Let's get those horses untacked and sponged off," Jody said as she walked by them to go into the house. "They've earned their break."

Christina reluctantly turned Sterling toward the barn. She untacked the mare and washed the sweat off in record time. Fortunately, Sterling was pretty cool after the long walk back from the far side of the cross-country field, so Christina didn't have to walk her any more before putting her into the stall. "Munch on this," she said, tossing a flake of hay over the door. "I promise to let you have some grass after quadrille practice."

By the time Christina and Melanie had finished with the horses and were jogging down the driveway, a couple of other campers, including Jennifer, had gathered at the ring to watch. The woman who had been leading Flash was just dismounting and talking to the man in breeches.

"Where's Eliza?" Christina asked Jennifer.

"I don't know. The last I saw of her was when Adrianne came to get her toward the end of our lesson. Why are those people riding Flash?"

Melanie nudged Christina. "I think we should tell her."

Jennifer's mouth dropped open as Christina quickly explained the situation to her. "You're kidding," she said.

Christina shook her head. "I wish I was."

"That must be the reason Eliza's been so touchy." Jennifer gave a disgusted sigh. "Well, that lady may own Flash, but she sure can't get him to move the way Eliza can."

They watched in gloomy silence as the man mounted, gathered up the reins, and began to walk Flash along the railing.

"He doesn't look like a very good rider, either," Christina said.

"You can say that again," Jennifer said as she put her arms on the fence and rested her chin.

It wasn't just his position, though his legs were poked out too far in front of him. There was something about the way he was holding his reins, something about how he sat up that made Christina feel his tension. Flash must have felt it, too, because he brought his head up higher and broke into a jig.

The man walked and trotted in both directions, his seat falling back heavily into the saddle every time he posted. By the time he asked for a canter, Christina could see the white part of Flash's eyes. The horse lunged forward, racing ahead as though he were trying to escape the man's heavy hands and seat. As soon as the man managed to pull Flash back to a walk again, he turned into the center of the ring and dismounted, shaking his head.

"I don't think he likes him," Christina said.

"Who? Flash or the man?" Jennifer quipped.

"Neither." Christina watched Lois run the stirrups up on both sides of the saddle and secure them so that they wouldn't bang against Flash's sides when he walked. Then she led him to the gate, glancing in the kids' direction as if she were looking for someone. Christina jogged over.

"Do you want me to take Flash for you?" she offered. "He's in the stall next to my horse."

"Would you?" Lois looked grateful. "I need to finish up some business here. Thanks," she said, passing the reins.

"Need some help?" Jennifer asked as she and Melanie fell into step beside her.

"Why don't you find Eliza and make sure she's all

right?" Christina glanced over her shoulder to make sure they were out of hearing range of Lois and the man. "And tell her we're pretty sure the guy doesn't want him."

As it turned out, Christina found Eliza first. She was picking out Flash's stall.

"I brought your horse back," Christina said, looking to see if she'd been crying. But Eliza's face was stony.

"Thanks," she said, tossing his halter over. "Would you mind untacking him while I finish up?"

"Sure," Christina answered, puzzled. Eliza didn't even act as if she were glad to see Flash.

When Eliza came back from dumping the muck bucket, she took over. Christina watched as she matter-of-factly sponged off the salt and sweat from his black coat.

"Well, aren't you even curious how it went?"

Eliza's hand paused, then she tossed the sponge back into the bucket. "Yeah, sure."

"The guy only rode about five minutes. I don't think he's interested."

Eliza snorted softly. "Yeah, well, there's always the next one."

"What do you mean?"

"I mean, Lois has got him advertised all over the place. She changed her mind about waiting until after camp is over to show him to people because she's found a mare she likes and she can't buy her until she has the money from Flash." Her words poured out. "And there's *nothing* I can do about it."

She untied Flash and led him toward the stream. Something about her back told Christina not to follow.

By lunch, everyone had found out about Flash. Eliza's seat was noticeably empty.

"I can't believe she's not going to be able to keep him," Rachel said. "They're perfect together."

"In the lesson this morning, Nathan said if Eliza and Flash kept it up, he wouldn't be surprised if they made the Young Riders team next year," Jennifer said.

"I'd just die if someone took Mushroom away from me," Anita added. "I know that I'm going to outgrow him some day—"

"You hope," Sean butted in.

Anita gave him a dirty look. "But at least when that times comes, I can decide who I want to sell him to."

Dylan wasn't saying much, but Christina could tell by the way he was staring at his plate that he was probably thinking about what it would be like to lose Dakota. She looked around the table. Everyone looked sad or mad—except maybe Sean, and you could never tell what he was really feeling. It didn't surprise her that they'd all be upset, though. Eventing was more than just riding. You had to develop a real partnership with your horse, or you'd never get anywhere. And it was hard to give up a partner.

"Why can't her parents buy Flash? They got her Cinders, didn't they?" Rachel said.

"They can't afford it right now."

"Maybe we can help her raise the money," Jennifer said. Christina shot Melanie a glance. Nobody but Perky and Uncle Will knew that the concert was being held to help Eliza. Christina thought that they should keep it a secret until they knew for sure how much money they were going to raise.

"We could sell food and stuff at the rock concert," Bekka suggested.

"Hot dogs. Get your hot dogs," Sean sang out.

Bekka hit him with her napkin. "They'd be too complicated. I'm talking about sodas and chips. My friend and I made enough money for our gymnastics trips selling stuff like that at the girls' soccer games."

"Yeah. We could buy bags of ice to keep the sodas cold," Dylan said.

Melanie hooted. "We could push them around in the wheelbarrows, just like sidewalk vendors—after we washed them out, of course."

Christina was warming to the plan. Even if they ended up having enough money from the concert's ticket sales alone to buy Flash, they could always donate any extra money to the camp.

"Who wants to help me find out about the sodas and stuff?" Bekka said.

"I will," Dylan said.

"Me too," Rachel added.

Sean jumped up. "I'll be in charge of making signs."

Christina smiled as everyone kept coming up with ideas. She'd better find Eliza and tell her the news.

Eliza was in the cabin.

"There you are," Christina said. "There's still some food left if you—" She broke off. "What are you doing?"

Eliza was throwing things into her trunk. "I can't stay now that everyone knows about Flash. I'm going home."

"You can't," Christina said. "Let me have that," she added, taking a blanket out of Eliza's hand. "We've got a plan."

Eliza listened to Bekka's idea about selling refreshments. "It would never make enough money," she said when Christina finished.

"Maybe not, but it's a start." Christina didn't want to tell her the rest of the secret until they saw how many people actually showed up at the concert. Besides, what if something went wrong? She remembered Uncle Will complaining that nothing was certain in the music business. They couldn't count on the money until the band was actually playing in the field.

"But now everybody knows about my father."

"No, they don't," Christina said. "And even if they did, it wouldn't matter. Like you told me, it wasn't his fault he was laid off."

Eliza just looked at her.

"Anyway, I told them Flash costs too much for

137

your parents to afford right now," Christina said. "Everyone can understand that."

Eliza's lower lip started to tremble. "What if Lois sells him before camp is over?"

Melanie and Jennifer burst into the cabin. "We'll horse-nap him and hold him for ransom," Melanie said.

Eliza actually smiled.

"We're a team, remember," Christina said, hanging her arm around Eliza's shoulders. Melanie and Jennifer joined the circle. "We need to stick together."

"Speaking of sticking together," Jennifer warned. "If we don't get our tails back to the barn to listen to Doc talk about horses and parasites, Dana will happily stick it to all of us when she totals up our points for the day."

On the way to the lecture, they stopped at the end of the barn to see if yesterday's points were posted yet. Team Three was now in last place.

"Man. That bit *was* clean," Melanie said, frowning at the note beside her name.

"Hay in front of Geronimo's door?" Jennifer read. "I swear the aisle was raked. He must have stuck his head out to look at something while he was still eating."

Christina looked over Melanie's shoulder. "Sweat marks behind Sterling's ears? Give me a break," she complained. "What am I supposed to do? Put in air-conditioning?"

Eliza raised her eyebrows as she looked at her

score. "Dirty brushes? Dana must have been in an especially bad mood last night."

Christina moved to the other teams' sheets. "Dylan's team only lost two points. And Anita's team didn't lose any."

Melanie snorted. "Dana really has it in for us, all right."

"Maybe we should complain to Ms. Perkins," Christina said.

Jennifer shook her head. "That will just get Dana madder. Let's face it. We're at her mercy."

Eliza agreed. "The best way to catch up is to come in first in our quadrille. And we better try to get on Dana's good side, too."

"How? By offering a bribe?" Melanie said out of the corner of her mouth.

Eliza laughed. "A granola bar or two wouldn't hurt."

Practicing the quadrille on foot last night might have helped some, but they still made mistakes during their afternoon practice.

"Wasn't Jennifer supposed to turn at B?" Melanie complained.

Nathan consulted the test. "Circle at B, then turn."

"O-kay," Melanie said, shrinking into her T-shirt. "Can we start again from the beginning?" she added in a small voice.

They ended up stopping a little early. But even after all that work, Sterling was hyper.

"I think he misses just going out on the trail," Christina said.

Eliza nodded. "You're probably right. The lessons are pretty intense." She called to Nathan. "Can we loop around the cross-country field and come back on the trail? Sterling needs a change of scenery."

Nathan considered it. "Promise you won't jump anything?"

"Promise," Eliza said.

"We'll just walk," Christina added.

He squinted through the trees. "I guess since Dana and Jody are out there with their teams, it would be okay. Just don't fall off."

"I'm going to head back to the barn," Jennifer said.

"I'm beat, too." Melanie dropped her stirrups and let her feet dangle. "Hey, Nathan. When we get back, can you show me how you taught Gulliver to bow?"

"They just want to have Nathan to themselves," Christina whispered as she and Eliza pointed the horses in the other direction.

"I know." Eliza rolled her eyes. "They are so obvious."

"What's that?" Christina said, halting Sterling.

"What?"

"That music. Where is it coming from?"

Eliza listened. "Over there, I think."

As they rode down the logging road past the stone wall that Sterling had soared over that morning, the music got louder.

"Hey. Stop spying on us," Sean called as they came into the field where another dressage arena with upside-down buckets was laid out. Dylan, Rachel, and Bekka were standing beside him and Dana was fiddling with something in the tall grass.

Eliza made a face. "Get a grip. We're just passing through."

Christina could feel Team Five's eyes as they rode past the arena and turned onto a trail.

"What was that all about?" Christina said.

"I guess they're going to do their quadrille to music," Eliza answered. "Dana had a boom box in the grass. I don't know why Sean's making such a big secret about it, though. I guess he's really worried about doing well."

Christina remembered about his family. "I'm surprised Sean doesn't tell his parents to get off his back," Christina said.

Eliza turned. "You haven't met his mother."

"Do you think we should try to do ours to music, too?" she said. "I don't want to lose to them just because their ride was fancier."

"We don't have time to do it right. And no judge is going to be impressed if we run into each other in time to the beat," Eliza said. "Don't worry about it."

"You're probably right," Christina said. Besides,

with the concert only four days away and still no word from Uncle Will about which group was coming so that they could start advertising, she had plenty to worry about already. Would anyone come on such short notice?

12

By Thursday afternoon, Christina felt as if she'd been at Saddlebrook Farm for a whole summer instead of less than a week.

"I think I could clean tack in my sleep," she told Eliza as she sat on her trunk, rubbing saddle soap into the rich brown leather of Sterling's bridle.

"It's working, though," Eliza said. "No lost points last night."

"Either that or Dana wants seconds on the box of cookies my mother sent," said Jennifer.

"Are you going to try calling your dad again?" Christina asked Melanie as they trooped up to the house for dinner. Rain was predicted for Sunday and they were trying to figure out what to do. Besides, he still hadn't let them know which group was coming. Christina was beginning to think it would be a miracle if they pulled this concert off.

Melanie nodded. "I'm going to tell him he needs a beeper."

They were finishing off what had been huge platters of taco salad when Melanie exploded out of Perky's office.

"He's sending Harvey and the Headknockers for our concert. They're the best! Ms. Perkins is calling the radio stations now. I wonder if we can get Channel Seven to announce it, too?"

Christina let out a huge sigh of relief.

"I've never even heard of them," Rachel said.

"That's because they only have two recordings so far, but they're really hot," Melanie said, dancing around a chair. "This fall, Dad's sending them on tour with Doomsday."

"Clear the way," Sean said, grabbing the pile of poster board and plopping it on the corner of the table. "We've got posters to make."

Right after breakfast on Friday, Christina, Melanie, and Jennifer rode into town with Perky to hang the posters and pick up the sodas and chips. Eliza didn't want to go. She was in a bad mood because her mother called to say that Eliza's dad wouldn't be coming to the Parents' Picnic because her little brother had made it into the all-star baseball team and had a game.

"I'll do this side of the street and you two take the

other," Ms. Perkins said. "When you put up all your posters, meet me at the grocery store."

Christina was studying the list Bekka had given her of the stuff they should buy when Ms. Perkins found them.

"I gave some posters to a friend who is on his way into Lexington this morning. He promised to post them for us." Even Perky sounded excited about the concert.

Ms. Perkins drove home slowly with the girls keeping an eye on the cases of soda piled in the back of the jeep. They didn't want them to tip over. On the way, they heard the concert announced on the radio.

"I hope a lot of people come," Christina said to Melanie.

"After all this work, they'd better."

It was after ten when they got back, just enough time before lunch for the two girls to join in their lesson.

On Saturday morning they had their final practice. The horses would have Sunday morning off. The team competition was scheduled for two o'clock Sunday afternoon.

"Dress rehearsal time," Melanie said as they walked the horses out to meet Nathan. "Break a leg."

"The way my luck's been going, I probably will," Eliza said, still stewing. "When I called my mother back to tell her she didn't have to come to our picnic if she wanted to watch Matt play, too, she jumped at the chance. She doesn't even care that this is probably the last time I'll get to compete on Flash."

Christina felt a stab of pity. Being an only child had its advantages.

After they warmed up, Nathan stood at the end of the arena. "Okay. Pretend I'm the judge and ride the test just like you're going to do it tomorrow."

Trib was too lazy, Sterling shied from the judge's box, and even Eliza messed up by turning down the center line too soon.

"Come on, guys," Jennifer complained. "We've got to do better than this."

They all tried, but even their best ride wasn't very good.

"Don't worry about it," Nathan said. "You just have dress rehearsal jitters. I'm sure it will go better tomorrow."

After lunch, he took them on a trail ride. It was exhilarating and Christina loved sailing over the jumps. Sterling was doing much better than she'd done during the practice.

After the girls put the horses away and were walking toward the kennels, Dana approached them with her usual scowl.

"Doesn't she ever smile?" Melanie whispered.

"Phone for you, Eliza."

"For me?" Eliza smiled. "Maybe Mom decided to come after all. Meet you back in the cabin."

Christina had just peeled off her hot boots and wet socks when Eliza came in.

"That was Lois," she said in a flat voice. "She's

bringing another person by to look at Flash tomorrow."

Jennifer swore out loud and Christina flopped back on the bed. "But the quadrille's tomorrow."

"She knows. They're going to come and watch, and if the lady likes what she sees, she'll try him afterward."

"That stinks," Melanie said. "How are you supposed to do a good job knowing that it might cost you your horse?"

"That's it," Jennifer said. When everyone looked at her, she explained. "All you have to do is make him look bad, then the woman won't be interested."

Melanie nodded her head. "Or if she is, maybe you could put something under his saddle somehow so when she got on, he'd buck."

Eliza rolled her eyes. "Get real," she said, vaulting onto her top bunk. "Like I'm really going to mess him up just so I can keep him longer."

"Why not?" Melanie asked. "It's not as if you're going to hurt him."

Christina nodded. "I don't know about the making him buck part, but if you want to blow the quadrille, I guess it's for a good cause."

Eliza stared at them. "That is the stupidest idea I've ever heard."

"We're just trying to help," Jennifer said, trying to keep the peace.

"Well, you're not, okay? It's bad enough that I'm going to lose Flash without you all coming up with all these stupid ideas." Eliza's eyes filled with tears. "I'm tired of getting my hopes up."

Her words were followed by silence. Even Melanie kept her mouth shut for once.

Christina touched Eliza's leg. "Want me to pull your boots off?"

Eliza nodded. As soon as they were off, she lay down on the bed with her face turned to the wall and her knees tucked to her chest.

When Christina woke up the next morning, she couldn't figure out what was making all the racket. Then she looked out the window at the water running off the metal roof. Oh no! It was raining.

Uncle Will had left it up to them to find a place indoors. Ms. Perkins lined up the high school gymnasium, but they would have to pay if they used it. And Christina knew not as many people would come to a concert in the high school.

Everyone was angry at the weather as they went about their morning chores, darting between the barns whenever the downpour let up a bit. Dylan stopped by Sterling's stall.

"How you doing?" he said, peeling the hood back from his poncho. His wet hair was plastered to his forehead.

Christina shook her head at the water streaming off the overhang. "I've been better."

"What?" The rain was so loud on the roof that Dylan had to lean closer.

"Have you heard a weather forecast?" she said.

Dylan nodded. "Don't worry. It's supposed to stop by lunchtime."

"Good." Christina could see tiny drops of water on his long dark eyelashes.

"Hey, you want to listen to the concert together?"

Christina smiled. "Sure."

"Okay," Dylan said, smiling back. "I'll see you there." He pulled his hood back on, then turned back. "Hey, good luck with your quadrille."

"Thanks. You too." As Christina watched Dylan run across the green, everything seemed a little brighter.

After breakfast, Ms. Perkins hauled out the left-over poster board and markers and began giving out assignments for the day's activities.

"We'll need to cordon off the barn area so that people coming to the concert won't wander through and disturb the horses. And we'll need plenty of PARKING and NO PARKING signs."

"I'll work on the ones for our refreshment stands," Rachel said. "Will you help me, Dylan?"

Melanie made kissy noises at Rachel's back, but Christina laughed, still warm inside knowing that Dylan had come out in the rain to ask *her* to sit with him at the concert.

Eliza just sat until someone shoved poster board

in front of her and told her to make NO SMOKING signs. She'd hardly said a word all morning. Christina knew she was still worried about the buyer Lois was bringing out.

By midday, the sun was starting to peek out through the last bits of rain. "A rainbow," someone shouted as Christina was helping hammer in stakes to wrap the bright orange plastic tape around. Christina looked up and smiled. The colors shimmering in the golden mist were a good omen.

After lunch, everything was in a uproar as campers raced around, trying to get ready.

"Can someone help me with this stupid net?" Christina said, whipping the black bow with its crocheted net off her ponytail. "My hair is too slippery. The ends keep coming out."

"Here," Eliza said, turning Christina so that she was facing away. "I've had a ton of practice."

"Christina!"

Christina's head jerked up. "Mom, Dad," she said, pulling away from Eliza's fingers. She ducked under the railing and ran toward her parents.

"I've missed you," she said, hugging them both at once.

"We've missed you, too," her mother said, squeezing her close. Christina inhaled the familiar smell of her father's shaving cream and her mother's green apple shampoo.

"It's been way too quiet at home," Dad said, his

hand giving her back one last pat as he pulled away. "Speaking of which, where's Melanie?"

Christina grinned up at him. "She's over here. Come on. I want you to meet everyone."

"Hi, Aunt Ashleigh, Uncle Mike," Melanie said as they swept her into a bear hug, too. "Have you seen Dad yet?" She pulled away, her eyes searching the green as it began to fill with parents.

"Didn't he call?" Christina's father was frowning.

Melanie shook her head.

Mike cleared his throat. "Well, the last I heard— and this was yesterday afternoon—he had some clients fly in unexpectedly and he wasn't positive he was going to be able to get away this weekend." He put his arm around Melanie. "So it looks like we'll have to cheer extra loudly for our girls."

When Melanie pulled away, Christina waited for her usual wisecrack answer. But Melanie just grabbed Trib's halter and lead shank and headed toward the stall without saying a word.

13

GREAT. JUST GREAT, CHRISTINA THOUGHT AS THEY SADDLED their horses. On one side of her, Eliza was as edgy as a cat as she watched for Lois and Flash's possible buyer. On the other side of Sterling, Melanie was slamming things around because Uncle Will might not show up after all. And further down, Jennifer was showing off for her boyfriend, Jason, who had come with her parents as a surprise. How were they ever going to be able to ride their quadrille well?

"We should be warming up right now." Eliza's voice was tense.

"I'm all set," Christina said, her worries taking a back seat as she admired Sterling. The mare's coat was brushed to a silver sheen and her mane lay in neat, even plaits down her long neck. "You ready, girl?" Sterling's wide, dark eyes gleamed as she lifted her head.

"We'll meet you over there," Jennifer said as Christina mounted.

Eliza rode by on Flash. "Don't take all day."

"Stuff it," Melanie muttered under her breath.

"See you in the warm-up ring," Christina said, eager to get away before World War III erupted.

The grass beside the dressage arena was dotted with blankets and folding chairs. Sterling shied as someone unfolding a blanket flapped it in the wind before letting it settle to the ground.

"Calm down, girl," Christina said, easily staying in the saddle as Sterling danced sideways. She turned into the fenced ring where half the kids were already warming up.

"Eliza," someone called. Christina looked behind her and saw Flash's owner waving with a smiling young woman in tow. Eliza rode Flash over to the fence and met them.

"Don't let us interrupt your warm-up," Christina heard the younger woman—Lois introduced her as Jane something—say to Eliza. She smiled as she shaded her eyes with her hand. "Just go ahead and do what you need to."

Sterling jigged and Christina dragged her attention away from the fence. If only Jane didn't sound so nice.

She was so busy concentrating on keeping Sterling from breaking into a jig every time they walked down the diagonal, she didn't notice that Melanie and

Jennifer had come in the ring until they appeared on either side of her.

"Let's practice our entrance," Jennifer said.

Melanie put the reins in her mouth and flung her arms open wide. "Ta da!" she said through her teeth.

Christina laughed, relieved that Melanie was back to her old self.

"You look great," Nathan said as he walked up. He glanced at his watch. "We're going to start in five minutes with Team One. Eliza," he called. "Over here."

They went through the beginning and end of the ride, making sure they were spread evenly into a fan as they halted. "You've warmed up enough," Nathan said. "Why don't you all relax and watch the first two rides?"

"I am so nervous," Jennifer said as they found a spot beside the driveway. "I wish I hadn't eaten those chips Jason brought."

"He's really cute," Melanie said. "How long have you been going out?"

Christina only half listened to Jennifer tell Melanie about her love life. She was glad Melanie got her talking, though, because it might keep her from getting nervous and choking up the way Eliza said she did last year. Christina's stomach didn't feel so hot, either, but she knew she'd feel better as soon as she rode Sterling into the arena.

Team One was the group Adrianne worked with. They were doing Introductory Quadrille Test 1, which didn't have any cantering. Anita had her work cut out for her, making sure Mushroom kept up with the rest.

"Look at that pony move," Jennifer commented when Anita pushed Mushroom into a lengthening down the long side so they'd reach the C marker in time for the crossover. "Do you think it will count against her for lengthening when the others are just doing a working trot?"

"I don't think it should," Christina said. "Not when she has to work with horses that are bigger than hers." She turned to Eliza. "Will it?"

Eliza wasn't paying attention. She was gazing off toward the A end of the arena.

Christina looked, too. Lois was talking and Jane was nodding. Both had their eyes on Flash.

Aside from the halt at the end of the first ride when one of the horses backed up two steps, Team One did a good job.

Team Two had chosen to ride Novice Quadrille Test 1, the same test as Christina's group. This ride wasn't nearly as even and smooth as Team One's. Poe had trouble getting Pork Chop to pick up the left lead canter, which threw off the spacing.

"Maybe we should have stuck to the introductory-level tests," Christina said to Eliza.

Eliza shook her head. "Don't picture what could go wrong, or it probably will. You need to think positively."

Suddenly, it was their turn. Christina gathered her

reins and squeezed Sterling forward, taking her number two spot behind Flash. She nodded at her parents, who grinned and waved from their blanket, then pushed Sterling alongside Flash for their entrance at A.

A thrill of excitement ran down Christina's arms as she and Eliza led the way. She could feel Sterling's back lift as the mare matched Flash's long, rhythmic stride. When they halted in an almost perfectly spaced fan formation to salute, Christina smiled at Frieda Bruder—who had gotten to the camp last night in time to judge—before dropping her head.

It was as if Sterling understood that it was time to pay attention. Christina could feel her softly mouthing the bit, waiting for Christina's next command when they split away from Flash at C. As Sterling proceeded down the long side, Christina watched Eliza out of the corner of her eye so that she could start their half circle after Flash's, ending up in single file going up the center line.

Jennifer and Geronimo were steady as they followed Flash, and Christina could hear Trib's sure footfalls behind her. Like clockwork, they ended up on the center line for a second before circling off again. Christina's heart swelled. It was as though they were dancing.

By the time they did their last crossover, Christina didn't have to try to remember to sit back and hold her chin high. Eliza nodded and grinned as she and

Flash met them one last time to turn down the center line and halt at G. Christina could hear her mother's piercing whistle after they saluted the judge.

"All right," Melanie said, giving Jennifer a high five.

Christina turned to Eliza. "Way to go, partner," she said.

Eliza leaned forward to pat Flash's neck. "Yeah," she answered with a catch in her voice. "Way to go, partner."

Christina's parents met them on the driveway.

"That was fabulous, honey," Ashleigh said.

Mike nodded. "Maybe you should give us a few dressage lessons. That was impressive."

"I've never seen Trib looking so good." Ashleigh patted Melanie's leg. "You guys have really clicked, haven't you?"

Melanie's smile quickly turned into a scowl. "Tell that to my father, will you, since he couldn't interrupt his busy schedule to come?"

"I know he wanted to see you, sweetie," Ashleigh said. "But sometimes business has to come first."

Melanie's eyebrows shot up. "Sometimes?"

Mike shook his head. "I'll try him again," he said, starting for the house. "Maybe his flight was delayed."

"Oh, I'm certain it was something unavoidable like that," Melanie said, not bothering to hide her contempt.

"Look," Jennifer said. "Team Five is getting ready to start."

Christina hadn't even seen any of Team Four's ride, but they had already finished and were dismounting. Team Five was waiting to go in with Bekka and Sean on one side of the arena, Dylan and Rachel on the other. The loudspeaker crackled, then rock music started pouring out.

"I knew it," Jennifer said.

Christina's stomach sank. She had felt so good about her team's quadrille. Now as she watched Bekka and Sean trot into the arena, their horses' strides in rhythm with the music, she felt defeated already.

Christina didn't recognize the test. "Which one are they riding?" she whispered to Eliza.

"It's a freestyle. They either made it up, or used the one that came with the tape."

"I hope they canter," Jennifer said. She had dismounted and was holding hands with Jason. "Poko doesn't like to pick up his right lead."

They did canter and everyone picked up the correct lead. But the music didn't match with their movements now. It was as though they were going faster than they should, but none of the horses were actually racing.

"This tape is for horses that are schooled at a higher level than these guys," Eliza explained. "Poko's and Jester's canters are too flat. They need to be collected more before they can get that slow, rolling motion."

They had to trot before the canter part of the music was over, and the two-beat rhythm of the trot didn't work at all with the three-beat music for the canter. Sean kept looking at Bekka as if it were her fault, and Dylan was trying to tell Sean to slow down a little so that the music could catch up to them. It was such a disaster that by the time they halted and saluted, Christina felt sorry for them.

Melanie laughed. "And we were afraid *they'd* win?"

Eliza shot her a look that said "shut up." "You wanted to use music, too, remember? We were just lucky that Nathan made us spend time on the basics instead."

"That was a lovely ride, Eliza," Jane said.

Christina hadn't even seen Lois and Jane come up.

Lois motioned for Eliza to get off. "She's going to try Flash now."

Jane's smile softened the order. "If you wouldn't mind."

Even though Jane was shorter than Eliza, she refused Lois's offer of a leg up and easily stretched her leg to the stirrup. Once she was on Flash's back, Christina could see that Jane could really ride.

Her arms looked like elastic as she brought Flash onto the bit, his back legs reaching far under his belly as he adjusted his stride in answer to her almost invisible commands. *She made him look as good as when Eliza rode him. Maybe even better,* Christina thought, feeling like a traitor.

Jane spent about ten minutes putting him through his paces before she halted by Lois and Eliza.

"I like him very much," she said to Lois.

Christina could see Eliza's body sag.

"I'm going to try another horse this afternoon. Can I let you know my decision by tomorrow?"

Christina's fingernails dug into her palms as Lois nodded. If they didn't make enough money at the concert tonight, it would be too late.

14

"WELL, AT LEAST THE BAND COULD MAKE IT," MELANIE said as two flatbed trucks rumbled up the farm drive-way. Uncle Will had finally called Melanie to say that he couldn't come after all. Now that the quadrille was over, the students and their parents were having a barbecue.

Christina took a mouthful of potato salad. Ashleigh put her hot dog down on the picnic table and wiped the mustard off her fingers before putting her arm around Melanie and drawing her close. "I know Will wanted to see you, honey. And he's promised to come to your event at the end of camp, hasn't he?"

"Not that his promises mean anything," Melanie said.

"But you've got to give him credit for organizing

this rock concert," Christina pointed out as two black vans with HARVEY AND THE HEADKNOCKERS painted on the sides followed the flatbed. "I mean, look at all that stuff."

Melanie shrugged. "Probably good for business," she said, swinging her leg over the picnic bench and getting up. "I'm going to find Jennifer and Jason."

"I'm sorry we can't stay for the concert, honey," Mike said.

"That's okay," Christina answered. "At least you got to see us ride."

"So, how's it been going?" Ashleigh asked. "You've been so surrounded by friends, I haven't had a chance to really ask you."

Christina considered everything that had happened in the week she'd been there. "It was a little hard at first," she admitted. "But once I started meeting people, it got better."

"Your roommates seem nice," her father commented. "Eliza is quite a good rider, too."

"Yeah, I know." She was about to tell them about Flash maybe being sold, when Ms. Perkins rang the dinner bell to get their attention. One by one, the groups of campers and parents at the picnic tables and blankets quieted.

"Would you like to hear the results of the quadrille before or after our make-it-yourself ice-cream sundaes?"

A loud chorus of "before" filled the air.

"Now why am I not surprised?" Perky said with a smile on her face. "What we saw today," she continued, addressing the parents, "was an example of the kind of teamwork we strive for at our clinic each year. Even though riding is primarily an individual sport, I believe that by working together we bring out the best in ourselves and our horses." She paused while everyone clapped.

"And now, the results of the quadrille rides, which, I might add, were all within seven points of the highest and lowest scores."

"That's pretty close," Christina whispered to her parents.

"In fifth place was Team Five," Ms. Perkins said. "And I'd like to commend Team Five for their courage in undertaking a difficult freestyle ride," she added, softening the blow of ending in last place. "I'm certain that their performance would have benefited greatly had they'd had more time to prepare."

As everyone clapped, Christina searched the crowd for Dylan. He was grinning good-naturedly as his mother squeezed his shoulders. Beside him, though, Sean and his mother were as stiff as statues.

"Fourth place goes to Team Two—"

Eliza slipped into the seat next to Christina as they waited to hear their team called.

"Third place is Team Four, with special recognition for their grooming."

"That was so cool the way they brushed the hair

165

on their horses' hindquarters to make them look like checkerboards," Christina said.

Eliza nodded, her fingers crossed.

"Second place goes to the team with the smallest four-legged member of our clinic, Team One."

Jennifer and Melanie erupted in war whoops across the yard as Christina realized that their team was the only one left. She and Eliza grabbed each other.

"And the winning ride belongs to Team Three, whose synchrony and alignment score was the highest of the day."

"I can't believe we won," Eliza exclaimed, bouncing in her seat as Melanie and Jennifer ran up.

"I can," Ashleigh said. "The four of you really communicated with your horses and each other."

"All that running around doing the quadrille on foot must have helped," Melanie said.

Eliza gave her a high five and smiled. "I guess we showed them."

All too soon, Christina waved to her parents as they drove down the driveway. For a second, she wished she were going home, too.

"Come on," Jennifer said. "The twenty-five points for winning the quadrille has pushed us into second place overall. If we want to win the team championship at the end of camp, we'll have to clean everything twice."

"'Cause we're the Four Musketeers," Melanie sang as she threw her arms over Christina's and Jennifer's shoulders.

"Come on, Eliza," Christina shouted.

Eliza joined in and they made a total spectacle of themselves as they strutted across the green.

"Pipe down," Dana said from her stall.

"Yes, sir," Melanie said, dropping one arm to salute. Christina jabbed her with an elbow. If they got Dana riled again, she'd never give them the points they deserved.

"What are you going to wear for the concert?" Melanie said as they trooped back to the cabin after evening chores.

"Shorts and a T-shirt, I guess," Christina said.

Melanie and Jennifer exchanged looks. "You're going out on a date with Dylan and you're just wearing regular stuff?" Jennifer said.

"It's not a date." Christina could feel her cheeks getting hot.

"Close enough," Melanie said.

They raided each other's trunks, giggling as they mixed and matched to assemble new outfits. The whole cabin was littered with clothes by the time they left, Melanie wearing Jennifer's halter top with her own painter's pants, and Jennifer wearing Christina's polo shirt tucked into Melanie's low-rise shorts. Even Eliza had gotten into the spirit of things, insisting that besides hiding Christina's scabs perfectly, her overalls would look great over Jennifer's close-fitted, striped T-shirt. For herself, Eliza had ended up with Melanie's Hard Rock Cafe shirt and a pair of cutoffs.

By the time they slipped into their places behind the refreshment stand, the parking lot behind the barn was full as people of all ages trooped past with their coolers and blankets.

"I didn't think about people bringing their own drinks and stuff," Christina said.

Melanie frowned. "Come on," she said to Jennifer.

"Where are you going?" Eliza asked.

"Hold the fort. We'll be right back," Melanie called over her shoulder.

Business had picked up by the time Jennifer and Melanie returned with freshly scrubbed horse buckets in each hand. They loaded two buckets with sodas and two with bags of chips and took off up the gently sloping hill where the crowd was waiting.

By the time the next group came to take over with the selling, the cash box was half full.

"You guys go ahead," Eliza said, looking happier than she had for days. "Since this is for Flash, I want to keep working."

"Look at how many tickets we've sold." Christina bent her head close to Melanie's. "I think Operation Flash is a success."

Dylan waved his arms. "Hey, Christina," he hollered. "Over here."

As they made a jagged line across the patchwork of blankets, little kids running around, and Frisbee games, the crowd started to roar. Christina looked at the flatbed trailers that were acting as a stage and saw somebody holding a mike.

"Hurry," she said, pushing Melanie. "They're about to start."

Dylan shifted to one side so that Christina could sit down. "Congratulations," he said. "You guys rode a great quadrille."

Christina brushed her hair out of her face. "Thanks," she said. "Your team looked great, too, until the canter."

"Don't remind me." Dylan rolled his eyes. "I told Sean we should have stuck to a walk trot test if we were going to use music."

"I think they're about to start." Rachel's hair brushed Dylan's shoulder as she leaned forward.

"Hey, maybe we can get together a quadrille team when we get home," Dylan said, still turned toward Christina. She could see a few freckles across his nose.

"That would be fun," Christina answered.

"Good." Dylan leaned so close, their shoulders bumped. "Everything's been so crazy, with the quadrilles and all, I feel like I've hardly had a chance to say more than hi since this clinic's started."

The crowd started cheering as five guys ran onto the stage, so Christina just smiled. As the band started playing, their heavy chords throbbing through the air, she felt herself soar with the music.

Melanie was right. Harvey and the Headknockers were good. By the time they'd started their third song, a whole group of people was dancing in front of the stage.

"You want to go down?" Dylan said, pointing to the dancers.

"Sure," Christina said, letting Dylan pull her to her feet.

Jennifer and her boyfriend came next, followed by Melanie and Sean. As everyone else from the camp came trickling down in twos and threes, they ended up dancing in a big group. But every time there was a slow song, Dylan came looking for Christina.

It was getting dark by the time the third slow dance ended. Christina started to move away, but Dylan tightened his arms, bending his head until their lips softly touched before letting her go.

It didn't feel like anything could go wrong now.

"Was that the greatest or what!" Jennifer said as she flopped on her bunk later that night. "Especially when everyone started dancing."

Christina grinned, remembering how soft Dylan's lips had felt. He had kissed her again when the concert was over, a longer kiss that still made her wobbly when she thought about it.

"We need to see about something," Melanie said, grabbing Christina by the arm.

170

"What?" Eliza's voice was muffled inside the oversized T-shirt she was pulling on for bed.

"Just something," Melanie sang in a mysterious voice. Christina remembered what the something was and hurried after her.

"Perky said we had to have lights off in a half hour," Christina said as she ran to catch up.

Melanie stopped. "Can *you* get to sleep before finding out if we sold enough tickets for Eliza to buy Flash?"

Christina burst out laughing. "No," she said. "Let's go."

The lights were still on in the kitchen of the big house. Christina knocked softly, then pushed open the door. "Ms. Perkins?"

A chair scraped back and Ms. Perkins appeared. "Christina? Melanie? Is anything wrong?"

"We just wanted to see if we could help count the ticket money." Melanie peered around Ms. Perkins. "Do you know how much we made?"

Ms. Perkins laughed. "I was going to wait until morning, but something tells me I'll not get you to bed until it's done."

Melanie rubbed her palms together. "Let me at it."

Christina had never seen so many ten- and twenty-dollar bills in her life. "Man oh man. Would I like to be let loose in a tack shop with this," she said as she put a rubber band around her bundle and added it to the pile. "Five hundred here."

Melanie did some quick calculations. "There's over five thousand dollars. And Bekka said we cleared at least six hundred fifty dollars on refreshments."

"With the two thousand dollars Eliza already has," Christina started.

"She has more than enough to buy Flash. Whoo-ee," Melanie shouted, jumping into the air. "We did it."

Christina and Melanie exchanged high fives, then danced around the room.

"Hold up, now."

Christina turned to Ms. Perkins. She wasn't smiling.

"We did it, we did it," Melanie sang.

"Girls, please."

"Sssssshhh," Christina said, jabbing her cousin to get her attention.

"What?" Melanie said. "Isn't it great?"

Ms. Perkins shook her head. "There seems to be some confusion here."

Melanie's smile faded. "About what?"

"About how this money will be used," Ms. Perkins said.

"What's so confusing about that? The money is going to Eliza so she can buy Flash. Right?" Melanie looked at Christina for confirmation.

"Oh, dear." Ms. Perkins sank back into her chair and closed her eyes.

Uh-oh, Christina thought. It felt as if something were pressing into her stomach.

Ms. Perkins sighed and turned to Melanie. "I'm afraid you're mistaken."

Melanie looked at her as if she were crazy. "What do you mean? I set it up, so I should know."

Ms. Perkins reached for the poster board sign that was stuck to the cardboard money box. "And what does this say?" Her voice was soft.

"Benefit Saddlebrook Young Riders." Melanie shrugged. "So what is Eliza, anyway? An old rider?" She laughed, but not like it was funny.

Christina stepped in. "You mean we can't use this money to buy Flash?"

Ms. Perkins looked as sad as Christina felt. "No. We can't."

"Why?"

"Because the concert was advertised as a benefit for the organization." She touched Melanie's arm. "It's what your father thought you wanted."

Melanie jerked her arm away. She stormed over to the wall and started hitting it. "That's *not* what I *told* him," she said, bursting into tears.

Christina rushed over. "Come on," she said, rubbing her cousin's back.

Melanie turned around and put her face on Christina's shoulder, sobbing.

"He never listens to me," she said with shuddering gulps. "He probably just heard the part about Eliza being here on a scholarship because she was such a good rider, and how she'll probably be on the

Young Riders team someday." Melanie stomped her foot. "He's always talking to other people when we're on the phone. I hear him whispering. He only half listens."

Christina led Melanie to a chair and helped her sit down.

"I thought you wanted to help the Young Riders program. I never dreamed you thought this money was being raised to buy Flash." Ms. Perkins's eyes looked teary, too. "If it were up to me, I'd buy that horse for Eliza in a second."

Melanie raised her head. "Then why can't you?"

"It's complicated," Ms. Perkins said. "Saddlebrook Young Riders is a nonprofit organization that's run by a board of directors. I'm hired to run the camp, but they are in charge of the money."

Melanie cradled her head in her hands. "I guess I'm always going to be a screwup."

Christina didn't know what to say.

15

AN HOUR LATER, CHRISTINA WAS WIDE AWAKE AS SHE LAY in bed. A moth kept flying into the screen by the light outside the cabin, but she didn't want to get up to turn it off because Melanie was finally asleep. She hadn't seen her cousin so down in weeks. Darn that stupid Uncle Will for getting things all mixed up. If you asked Christina, he was failing miserably as a parent, which was pretty sad considering he was the only parent Melanie had.

She guessed she must have fallen asleep for a while, because when she opened her eyes it was getting light outside. Christina pushed the button on her watch. The green numbers showed five forty-five.

Christina kicked off her sheet. It was so muggy, her legs felt sticky already. She was sick of her bed, sick of the tossing and turning. She wanted to be with Sterling.

She carried her sneakers in her hand as she opened the screen door slowly so that it wouldn't squeak. At least it was a little cooler outside, she thought as she jammed her feet into her sneakers and headed to the barn. She hoped she wouldn't run into Gus on the way. They weren't supposed to be near the barns for another hour.

Christina held her hand up in the air to draw the gnats away from her face. Pesky things. When her arm got tired, she dropped it and jogged the rest of the way almost on tiptoe so that she wouldn't rouse anyone.

The horses knew she was coming, though. Christina could hear hungry nickers as she rounded the corner.

"Hi, Pork Chop," she said softly. "Go back to sleep. Breakfast isn't ready yet."

Sterling was waiting, too, and as Christina got closer, the mare kicked the door.

"Sssh," Christina said, pushing Sterling back so that she could slip into the stall. Sterling dropped her nose to Christina's bare legs and sniffed. Her whiskers tickled.

"Do you mind?" Christina reached up and scratched Sterling behind one ear until the mare closed her eyes and twisted her head in bliss.

"Oooooh, you like that, don't you, girl?" she murmured as Sterling leaned in toward her. "It doesn't take much to make you happy." Christina sighed. She wished life could be that simple for people, too. Then Eliza wouldn't feel so terrible when Flash was sold.

"I could never lose you," Christina said, laying her

cheek in the warm place where Sterling's neck and shoulder joined. "I'd beg, borrow, or steal before I'd let anyone take you away from me."

She closed her eyes, drinking in Sterling's special hay, sawdust, and shampoo smell, when her words hit her. Borrow. That was it! Maybe they could borrow the money they had raised to buy Flash.

By six-thirty, Christina couldn't hold off any longer. She had to see Perky.

"Good morning," Ms. Perkins said as she answered Christina's knock.

"Could we talk?" Christina said, glad that Ms. Perkins didn't mind being disturbed so early.

"Certainly. Come right in. I was just fixing myself a cup of tea. Would you like some orange juice?"

"No. I mean, no thank you." Christina tried to organize what she wanted to say.

"Ms. Perkins, if those people who decide what to do with the money we made from the concert *really* want to help build up a strong Young Riders team, then why can't they give Eliza a loan so she can buy Flash?"

Ms. Perkins turned and stared.

"She's saved up a lot of money already." Christina raced on before Ms. Perkins could open her mouth. "And it wouldn't have to be like the scholarship she got to come to the camp. I mean a *real* loan—one that she could pay back slowly. She's a hard worker."

Ms. Perkins smiled. "I know she's a hard worker. But five thousand dollars is a lot to pay back."

Christina bit her lip as she thought. "Well, she baby-sits a lot. And couldn't she work some of it off being a junior counselor?"

"I've thought about that. Of course, we usually require the juniors to be sixteen, but given these circumstances, maybe a month or two wouldn't matter." Ms. Perkins sighed. "Even so, she would only earn five hundred dollars as a counselor."

When Christina's eyes fell on the *Practical Horseman* lying on the table, she got another idea. "What if Saddlebrook bought him for Eliza to use?" She pointed to the horse on the cover of the magazine. "Tidal Wave is owned by a company, isn't he? But Alexis Dean competes him and takes care of him just like he was her own horse."

"I don't know," Ms. Perkins said, slowly shaking her head. "That might be even trickier."

Christina was getting desperate. "But Eliza and Flash belong together. You know they do. There must be *something* you could do to help."

Ms. Perkins pursed her lips as she looked out the window. Christina held her breath, wondering if she had said too much.

"You've brought up some interesting possibilities," Ms. Perkins finally said. Her long fingers drummed the table as she thought some more. "With the cost of horses these days, we really need to come up with creative solutions for our riders."

She looked at Christina and smiled. "I'm going to

make a few phone calls. Most of our directors will be in their barns right about now, anyway."

Christina let out her breath. "Thank you."

Ms. Perkins held up her finger. "I'm not making any promises, now, so don't get your hopes up. And don't talk to Eliza yet."

"I won't."

"Then run along now to your chores and I'll see what I can do."

Christina kept one eye on the house as she fed Sterling and cleaned her stall, but Perky didn't appear. When she saw Ms. Perkins at breakfast, the woman shrugged and shook her head slightly.

Everybody was quieter than usual, probably tired from being up so late at the concert. Eliza hadn't touched her pancakes. Even Sean was subdued. Christina remembered how mad his mother looked yesterday when the quadrille scores were announced. Was that why he looked so down?

The telephone rang as Christina leaned closer to Dylan to ask if Sean was okay.

"Eliza. It's for you." Ms. Perkins beckoned from her office.

Eliza's face was ashen as she got up from the table. "I know it's going to be Lois," she said. She walked into the office as though she were heading to the guillotine. The door closed behind her.

"That was fun last night," Dylan said, his brown eyes looking down at Christina. She blushed, remembering their kiss. For a second, she forgot what she was going to say, but Dylan was still talking.

"Now that Frieda Bruder's here, we'll have four lesson groups instead of three. Maybe we'll get moved into the same class."

Christina thought about how much she had learned from Jody. She wasn't sure she even wanted to switch anymore.

"We'll be jumping most every day now, since we have to get ready for the event at the end of camp," Dylan continued. "Kevin said he wouldn't be surprised if you and Sterling went in the higher division."

"Really?" Christina knew the camp event was broken down into more divisions than regular events, but before Christina could ask how high they would jump, Ms. Perkins called her into the office. "And bring Melanie, too."

Eliza was putting down the phone when they walked in. Her mouth was open as if she were in shock. When she saw them standing there, she gave her head a little shake and her whole face lit up.

"That was my parents. Flash is going to be mine," she said in disbelief. Then, with a squeal, she put her hands on either side of her head and twirled around.

"Ya-hoo," Melanie hollered, joining in the dance. Before Christina knew what was happening, she was pulled in, too.

"We're going to get the money from Saddlebrook's Young Riders fund. It'll be like a student loan," Eliza said, hopping from one foot to another. "Mom and Dad will sign the papers, but it will be my responsibility. My first payment isn't even due until next summer, but I can send baby-sitting money before then."

Christina had never seen Eliza so happy.

"And guess what? I'm going to be a junior counselor next summer. They're bending the rules a little, since I'm almost going to be sixteen. Hey, maybe you guys will be in my barn."

"Bending the rules?" Christina teased, remembering when Eliza accused her of getting special treatment just because of her parents.

"Thank you," Eliza said, reaching out to take Melanie's and Christina's hands. "If it wasn't for you two, I would never have been able to buy Flash."

"But you did it, too," Christina said. "Ms. Perkins wouldn't have set this loan up if you and Flash weren't such good partners."

"We all did it," Melanie sang out, dancing in a circle. "We did it, we did it."

Jennifer stuck her head around the corner. "What on earth is wrong with you guys?"

"Nothing's wrong," Eliza said, pulling her into the fray.

Two more weeks of camp. Two weeks packed with riding and friends.

"Everything's right, now," Christina said, grinning at her team. "Everything."

DALE BLACKWELL GASQUE has ridden and trained horses most of her life. As a teenager, she showed in equitation and hunter classes before combined training events caught her interest. After spending time in England earning her British Horse Society assistant instructor degree, she bought her first Thoroughbred off the track and reschooled her as a dressage and event horse.

Ms. Gasque is an elementary school librarian who says the best part of her job is finding good books for kids to read. When she's not in school or at her computer writing horse stories, chances are she's eventing Christopher Robin, her latest ex-racehorse, or trail riding with her husband and two children on their Vermont farm in the mountains.

created by Joanna Campbell

Read all the books in the Thoroughbred series and experience the thrill of riding and racing, along with Ashleigh Griffen, Samantha McLean, Cindy McLean, and their beloved horses.